THE LANTERN OF LOST MEMORIES

Sanaka Hiiragi was born in 1974 in the Kagawa Prefecture. She graduated from Kobe Women's University, majored in literature and completed her studies at Himeji Dokkyo University. After living and working overseas as a Japanese language teacher for seven years, her debut novel, *The Battle of Marriage Island*, was nominated for the Konomys Award in 2012 and was chosen as 'The Hidden Jade' by the editors in 2013. She is a big fan of cameras, photography and kimono art.

The Lantern of Lost Memories

SANAKA HIIRAGI

Translated from Japanese by Jesse Kirkwood

PICADOR

First published 2024 by Picador

This paperback edition published 2025 by Picador
an imprint of Pan Macmillan
The Smithson, 6 Briset Street, London EC1M 5NR
EU representative: Macmillan Publishers Ireland Ltd, 1st Floor,
The Liffey Trust Centre, 117–126 Sheriff Street Upper,
Dublin 1 D01 YC43
Associated companies throughout the world

ISBN 978-1-0350-2363-9

Copyright © Sanaka Hiiragi 2019
Translation copyright © Jesse Kirkwood 2024

Originally published in Japan as 人生写真館の奇跡
by Takarajimasha Japan in 2019.

The right of Sanaka Hiiragi to be identified as the
author of this work has been asserted in accordance
with the Copyright, Designs and Patents Act 1988.

1 3 5 7 9 8 6 4 2

A CIP catalogue record for this book is available from the British Library.

Typeset by Palimpsest Book Production Limited, Falkirk, Stirlingshire
Printed and bound in the UK using 100% Renewable Electricity by CPI Group (UK) Ltd

Visit **www.picador.com** to read more about all our books
and to buy them.

Contents

Contents

Chapter One

The Old Lady and the Bus

The hands and pendulum of the old wooden clock on the wall were motionless. Hirasaka cocked his head to listen, but the silence inside the photo studio was practically deafening.

His leather shoes sank softly into the ageing red carpet as he made his way over to the arrangement of flowers on the reception counter. Carefully, he adjusted the angle of the petals.

At the back of the foyer, a pair of double doors opened onto the photo studio. In the dimly lit interior, an elegant chaise longue stood in front of a paper backdrop. Nearby, a large bellows camera had been positioned on a tripod made, like the camera itself, from sturdy-looking wood.

The contraption seemed far too big for a single person to carry – much to the amazement of Hirasaka's guests, who never failed to comment on its unique appearance. Those who knew a little about photography would say something along the lines of: 'Ah, is that an old Anthony?' before getting into a lengthy discussion about cameras.

Just then, a figure flitted by the window, and a voice called out, accompanied by a series of jolly-sounding knocks at the door.

'Delivery for you, Mr Hirasaka!'

Marvelling at the delivery man's ability to remain so chipper as he repeated this same task over and over, Hirasaka opened the door.

Outside stood a young man in the uniform of a delivery company, his cap tilted back, the usual trolley at his side. When Hirasaka saw the size of the package on top, he practically gasped.

On the delivery man's chest was a logo of a white cat, alongside a name badge that read *Yama*. His shaved head and tanned arms seemed somehow to complement each other.

'Looks like today's guest is a charming young woman,' grinned Yama, holding out his clipboard.

'Hah. Nice try,' said Hirasaka with a wry smile as he signed for the delivery.

'Mind giving me a hand? Been a while since I've delivered a package this heavy! Must be a hundred years' worth of photos here, I reckon.'

With a coordinated grunt, the two men heaved the large package onto the reception counter. Hearing Hirasaka let out a sigh, Yama turned and said: 'So, finally thinking about quitting, then?'

'One day, maybe. But I think I'll stick at it a little longer.'

'Never one to give up, are you!' said Yama, straightening his cap. 'Well, I should get going. Deliveries to make, and all that. Rushed off our feet, aren't we? One of these days we'll work ourselves to death!'

'Oh, I'd say that's the one thing we *don't* need to worry about.'

With a little wave, Yama tucked his clipboard under his arm and set off again with the trolley.

Hirasaka began preparing the room for his next guest. Her name, he saw, was Hatsue Yagi. He hoped he could give her a good send-off, with just the right photos to see her on her way.

And, more than anything, he hoped that one day, he'd finally meet that *somebody* he was waiting for.

——— • ———

'Hatsue? Hatsue Yagi?'

Hearing a voice gently calling her name, the old lady woke with a start.

Where was she? She appeared to be lying on her side on a sofa. Above her was an unfamiliar ceiling, and in front of her was a man, peering at her with a worried expression.

Could she have collapsed from heat stroke? It *had* been very hot recently. But when she tried to recall what had happened, her memories were hazy.

Let's see, my name is Hatsue. I'm ninety-two, and I was born in Toshima, Tokyo.

Phew, she thought. *Looks like I haven't lost the plot completely.*

Still, she felt a pang of worry as she stared at the man's face. *If he knows my name, then he must be an acquaintance of some sort. But who . . .? Or did he just find my name among my things?* Sifting through her memories, she began to sit up on the sofa, slowly raising her body while trying to avoid straining her lower back. For someone who'd just collapsed, her body seemed in decent enough shape.

Really, though. Who is he? Normally, even if someone unexpectedly greeted her on the street, she would eventually remember who they were and, to their delight, exclaim, 'Oh, it's you!' She concluded, with some exasperation, that she must finally be going senile.

'Welcome. I've been waiting for you!' said the man.

When she pointed at herself, as if to confirm that he meant her, he nodded.

'Mrs Hatsue Yagi, yes?'

'Erm, yes . . .'

She glanced up. The man was smartly dressed in a grey shirt with a stand-up collar, giving him the air of a good-natured vicar or priest, and his hair was neatly coiffed. He seemed kind, at least from his appearance, but there was also something a little mysterious about him. He wasn't strikingly handsome, but nor was he ugly: his face was unremarkable, and yet somehow vaguely familiar.

'My name is Hirasaka,' said the man. 'I run this photo studio – and have done for quite some time.'

Come to think of it, where was her cane? Had she dropped it when she collapsed?

As Hatsue glanced around the room, the man launched into an explanation of her surroundings.

'Those doors on the left lead to the main studio. Photos can also be taken in the courtyard. On the right is the waiting room and workshop. Please, come on in, and I'll show you around.'

Hatsue's mind was buzzing with questions, just like it always was.

What did he mean when he said he'd been 'waiting' for me?

What does the owner of a photography studio want with me, of all people?

And how did I even get here?

She couldn't remember a thing.

'This way, please,' said Hirasaka. She decided to set her questions to one side, and cautiously got to her feet. It had been a while since she'd walked without her cane. Leaning on the sofa to take the strain off her legs, she began shuffling along. Strangely enough, her entire body felt much better than it had in a long time, and her usual lower back pain had disappeared entirely. Hirasaka turned and, with a kind look, offered his arm.

He led her to a calm, comfortable-looking waiting room. The leather sofa was worn but well buffed, and the aged wooden desk was equally charming. Hatsue sensed that these choices of furniture resulted not from some lavish attachment to antiques, but rather from a habit of looking after things properly. Clearly, the young man had refined tastes for his age.

Through the window she could see a courtyard, lit by a small, flickering lamp. Peering closer, she was struck by the elegant sight of moss-covered stone lanterns, weeping cherry trees and the yellow flowers of a tsuwabuki plant. Not a bad background for a kimono photo, she thought.

In one corner of the waiting room was a cabinet on which an electric kettle, a siphon coffee maker and various cups had been arranged. Hirasaka must be diligent about cleaning, thought Hatsue – there wasn't a speck of dust to be seen. On top of the desk, a large box caught her attention.

'I'll make you some tea,' said Hirasaka and, turning away from her, set about preparing a teapot with well-practised movements. Watching him from behind, Hatsue decided it was time to ask the question that had been weighing on her mind.

'Erm, excuse me!'

Hirasaka turned to face her.

'Sorry to ask such an odd question, but . . .'

'Please, go ahead.'

'Am I . . . I mean, could I by any chance be . . . dead?'

Hirasaka's eyes widened slightly.

'. . . Yes. You died just now, in fact. This is normally when I start explaining the situation. But every now and then, a guest works it out all on their own – like you just have.'

At this no-nonsense response, Hatsue felt a strange mixture of relief and bewilderment – not to mention pride in her deductive skills.

The tea was perfectly brewed – neither too strong, nor too weak.

She had thought that being dead would feel a lot more like, well, being dead. She'd have one of those traditional triangular cloths placed on her head, or her body would have turned transparent. But no, there was nothing remotely ghostly about her. The feeling of the teacup in her hands, the flavour of the tea . . . everything seemed exactly as it had when she was alive.

Hirasaka sat down in the chair opposite and gazed steadily at her.

She couldn't help voicing her thoughts. 'But . . . I always thought that when I reached the afterlife, I'd find everyone waiting. My mother and father. My husband . . .'

Instead, she'd been greeted by this Hirasaka person, a complete stranger.

'Oh, don't worry,' he said, reassuringly. He must have noticed the glum look on her face. 'This is just a brief stop along the way.'

'Say, Mr Hirasaka,' she said, after a moment's reflection. 'I don't suppose your name has something to do with Yomotsu Hirasaka?'

Hirasaka's eyes widened again. Yomotsu Hirasaka was the name of the slope that separated the world of the living from that of the dead, down which the deity Izanagi was said to have ventured in search of his wife.

'Wow, Hatsue! You really do know your stuff.'

With her natural curiosity and love of reading, Hatsue had all sorts of facts like this at her fingertips. Looks like I've not gone soft in the head just yet, she thought to herself proudly.

'You're right, it does. Well, that should speed things up. You see, this place is located at precisely that boundary between life and death.'

'And your job is to greet me here?'

'Yes. Although this is really just a sort of staging post.'

'You mean I'm not in the afterlife proper?'

'No, not yet.'

'And does that make you . . . Enma, the King of the Underworld? Some kind of god? Buddha? I mean, you—'

With Hirasaka sitting there so quietly, beaming at her like that, she wanted to finish her sentence: *You don't exactly look the part*. With a cup of tea in his hands, he looked very much the ordinary human.

'Oh, no. I'm just a guide of sorts. See, when you go around telling people they've died, they tend to start crying, or getting a little depressed about it. Some of them make quite a scene. My job is to soften the blow slightly. That's why this photo studio is designed to feel as similar to the world of the living as possible.'

Hatsue glanced around. It was true that the place resembled nothing more than a quiet photo studio. If she *had* been hauled in front of the King of the Underworld all of a sudden, she'd probably have been shaking too much to even say a word.

'That's also why you're wearing your normal clothes.

The idea is that even on the outside, you look like the same old you.'

'I do like how my knee is all better,' she said, bobbing her leg up and down. Hirasaka nodded approvingly.

'If you run, you'll still break a sweat and get out of breath. You're essentially still inhabiting the same body you had when you were alive.'

Hatsue tried opening and closing her hand. He was right; everything felt just as it always had. It was hard to believe this body of hers no longer existed.

'And where do I go after this, then? To the afterlife?'

If that's where I'm going, then so be it. But at least let me know what's going to happen next.

'That's right. But first, there's a little something I need you to do for me.'

What could that be, she wondered?

Hirasaka scrabbled around inside the large box on top of the desk. Then he began producing a series of small bundles, each containing what looked like a stack of white paper. They were too big to hold with one hand, and seemed almost endless in number.

'What are those, then? Where are my reading glasses? I can't see a thing without them.'

'Actually, you should be just fine without them,' replied Hirasaka. 'Try really focusing.'

She looked down at the bundles in front of her and found

that her vision, normally so blurry, snapped into focus. She could see perfectly. It was a long time since she'd been able to take in so much detail with her naked eyes.

'Ah . . .' said Hatsue as she realized what the pieces of paper in front of her were.

They were photos. Hundreds and hundreds of photos, depicting all sorts of scenes from her life. The square near her childhood home, her mother and father when they were younger . . . Who could have taken them? The photos were a bit larger than normal photos, and had a pleasant feel.

'These, Hatsue, are the photos of your life. One for every day, three hundred and sixty-five for every year. And you lived to a whopping ninety-two, which makes for quite the collection . . .'

Hatsue started leafing through the photos one by one. As she did so, all sorts of things she'd forgotten came back to her. The warbling white-eyes that perched in the persimmon tree outside her family home. That old slatted box they used to keep the milk bottles in. The light slanting through the lattice door to their home, creating beautiful striped patterns on the floor.

'You've got all the time in the world, so please take as long as you need. I'd like you to pick out ninety-two photos, one for every year you were alive. Whichever ones you like.'

'But . . . whatever for?'

Hirasaka opened a door on the right to reveal a work-bench and, alongside it, a curious wooden contraption. In the middle of it was a round tray which looked like it was intended to carry something. This was supported by four columns which extended down to a sturdy-looking base. She could also see a thin bamboo pole and something that resembled a pinwheel. The wood had not been varnished or painted, and the entire assemblage looked as though it were still under construction.

'The photos you pick will be attached to this spinning lantern.'

Hatsue seemed to freeze.

'Wait. Is this the "lantern of memories" you're supposed to see before you die? Your life flashing before your eyes, and all that?'

'Yes, that's the one.'

'You mean I . . . get to choose the photos myself?'

'That's right.' Hirasaka grasped the wooden frame gently as he spoke. 'Each of my guests selects their favourite photos, and they end up on this lantern.'

'I had no idea it was a do-it-yourself sort of thing . . .' said Hatsue, still in shock.

'With all these photos, I imagine the lantern itself will be a real work of art. I'll be looking forward to showing you your life, Hatsue. All ninety-two years of it.'

Hatsue had always thought the 'spinning lantern' was just a metaphor – a way of talking about the rush of memories people experienced before they died. She never imagined it might be something you actually built.

'So when someone has a near-death experience and says they saw their life flash before their eyes, this is what they mean?'

'Yes. In some rare cases, people arrive here only to return, eventually, to the world of the living. But it seems they forget they were ever here, or that they chose the photos themselves. All they remember, vaguely, is the lantern of memories. Now, please have a look in here.'

Hirasaka led her back into the foyer, where he opened a door on the other side to reveal a perfectly square room. Peering in, she saw that not only the walls, but also everything else in the room, including the floor and a comfortable-looking sofa, was pure white. It looked like some kind of art installation. Hatsue could also see a door on the right which appeared to lead outside.

'This room is for the final stage of proceedings, when we light the lantern. It's a show designed for one person only, and that's you. Though I'd be very happy if you'd let me sit in on the viewing, so I can enjoy the fruits of our labour.'

The spinning lanterns Hatsue had seen in the past had been made from delicate, floral-patterned Japanese paper, with a red or yellow light in the middle. She remembered gazing at them as they slowly revolved.

'I have to say, getting to the afterlife is a little more complicated than I expected. I always thought you just sort of popped across the Sanzu River . . .'

'Think of it as a sort of final ceremony. A chance to look back on your life.'

Hatsue decided this was as good a time as any to ask the other question that was on her mind.

'You said this was a sort of staging post. So, where do I go after this?'

Hirasaka dropped his gaze for a moment, before glancing back up. He seemed to be trying to find the right words.

'I'm afraid I don't know. All I've heard are rumours. I haven't made it to the afterlife yet either, you see. Nobody who has ever comes back.'

This was a little disconcerting. What kind of place was the afterlife, then? Or was she just going to sort of . . . fade away?

'What I *have* heard,' he continued, 'is that souls who successfully pass into the afterlife are reborn. In other words, they get to live a whole new life.'

They returned to the waiting room, where Hirasaka poured them each a fresh cup of tea.

Hatsue brought the cup to her lips. As she drank, she

thought to herself: *This tea is just the right temperature, but I suppose dying means losing my awareness of things like that. Forgetting everything I've ever known. My consciousness slowly vanishing.*

'Even once you pass into the other world, it's not like everything that makes you Hatsue disappears completely. You see, our souls are a sort of repository for the accumulated memories of generations.

'For example,' he continued after a short pause, 'say you meet someone for the first time, but you're convinced you've met them before. Or you feel like you know a place even though you've never been there. I'm sure you've experienced that kind of thing in the past?'

'Oh yes,' replied Hatsue. 'In fact, even this photo studio feels strangely familiar.'

'That might be one of the memories that has accumulated in your soul, then,' replied Hirasaka with a smile. 'On the other hand, if an intense emotion ties you to the world of the living – a lingering regret, for example, or a long-held resentment – it can be impossible to make it to the afterlife. When that happens, your soul ends up trapped in one place.'

Hatsue nodded.

'So, Mr Hirasaka, what you're saying is . . . I choose some photos – ninety-two of them, one for each year of my life – and help you build a lantern out of them. Then

I'll watch that lantern spin, and depart in peace for the afterlife?'

Sounds like I have my work cut out for me, she thought. Death was turning out to be an exhausting business.

'Yes. You see, once you get here, it doesn't matter how wealthy or important you were in life. All you're left with are your memories.'

Hatsue stared at the enormous pile of photos in front of her. Just how long was it going to take her to get through them all?

'Funny,' she said, 'I didn't expect to be making the thing by hand. These days it's all computers and smart-phones!'

Hirasaka extracted a single photo from the pile.

'Well, let's see what you make of this one, for example. Do you remember this place?'

The photo he handed her showed a sloping road.

'Ah . . .'

She remembered.

On either side of the road that ran down the middle of the photograph, rice paddies stretched as far as the eye could see. A gust of wind was sending ripples through the rice plants, like waves on some vast sea.

She remembered the sweat dripping from her temples as she ran down the slope. A dry wind blowing. The salty taste on her lips. Ahead of her a heron, startled, taking flight, growing smaller and smaller in the sky until it was nothing but a white dot. She had watched until it disappeared completely, the sleeves of her kimono fluttering, the wind suddenly a roar in her ears.

Yes, she remembered. That summer when she was still young, a summer so long it seemed endless. Her body brimming with energy. The feeling she could run down that slope for ever.

'Bringing back any memories?'

'. . . Oh, yes. That road led through the paddy fields to the nearest town. I used to love walking along it.' Just taking the photo in her hand had been enough to trigger a wave of memories and emotions.

'And was it somewhere you remembered before seeing the photo?'

'No, not in the slightest. I'd forgotten it even existed. That whole area was paved over and turned into housing, you see.'

Hirasaka took the photo and inspected it himself.

'It *is* a lovely view.'

'Yes. Even if it doesn't exist any more.'

Hirasaka silently handed the photo back to her. 'When you look at this photo, I suppose all sorts of other things come back to you. Your memories from the time it was taken.'

Examining the photo more closely, Hatsue noticed how

grainy it was. The photo was really only a mass of tiny dots, and yet within its four corners it seemed to contain everything important about the day it was taken – the rush of the wind, everything she'd heard and felt . . . How was it possible for all that to be hiding among those specks of colour?

'Photos do have a certain power, don't they?' said Hirasaka quietly.

Hatsue was still gazing at the photograph. It was no work of art – just a photo of a country road. But now that the scenery shown in it had disappeared for ever, it had become the one place where it could still be found. To Hatsue, this ordinary-looking photograph suddenly seemed incredibly precious.

With Hirasaka's encouragement, Hatsue leaned forwards and set about choosing her photos, taking one after another from the pile. Because she found herself gazing at each of them for a long time, it was pretty slow going.

As she carefully leafed through the photos, she realized that, all things considered, she had really forgotten quite a lot. With some things, she'd even forgotten that she'd forgotten them – although, now that she thought about it, that was how forgetting worked. Until she looked at each photo, she'd have no recollection of the object or scene it showed, but then, in an instant, it would all come back to her.

Apparently not wanting to be a nuisance, Hirasaka told her she could ask him anything at any time and withdrew to an appropriate distance. Even when he went off to work on the lantern he left the door open, as if to keep a friendly eye on her. Perhaps because of the large number of photos it was designed to accommodate, the lantern was quite an elaborate construction, and would be difficult for a single person to carry. Yes, she thought, ninety-two photos probably would make for an impressive show.

Looking through the photos was quite a tiring process. When she glanced at the box, still full of bundle after bundle of them, she couldn't believe the scale of the task ahead.

When she'd got as far as age seven, Hirasaka came over.

'Is this your selection?' said Hirasaka, glancing at a stack of photos by her side.

'I thought I'd go through and make a shortlist, then whittle that down to the final ninety-two. But I have to admit I'm feeling a little overwhelmed!'

'Please feel free to take a break at any time. Your body won't tire, but your mind might.' He paused. 'Can I have a look?'

'Of course, feel free,' she replied. She felt strangely shy, as if she were showing him an album of photos she'd taken herself.

'Are these your parents? They look very kind.'

Her father was wearing a waistcoat; her mother, standing by his side, wore an old-fashioned smock over her kimono. In her hand was a Western-style umbrella. There must have been rain forecast that day. In her other hand was a basket. Ah yes, remembered Hatsue. They always used to take a bamboo basket like that with them when they went shopping.

'And these must be your friends from the neighbourhood.'

Little Mii-chan from next door was in front, gleefully showing off the gaps where her baby teeth had been; behind her, with their shaven heads, were the three Tagawa brothers. Their short trousers, frayed at the hems and patched in places, would have been hand-me-downs of hand-me-downs. Back then, people fixed things when they wore out, and that applied to clothes, too.

'That's right. I was the fastest out of all the local kids, good at swimming, and knew how to hold my own in an argument, so the adults always called me the leader of the pack. Told me I'd never find a husband if I carried on that way. Look at the state of us – I don't remember looking that filthy!'

Hirasaka chuckled.

Hatsue glanced down at the photos spread across the desk. 'But you see, I really have forgotten all sorts. Even things I thought I remembered perfectly well. I found myself gazing at my parents' faces for the longest time before it clicked!'

She'd forgotten all about that favourite picture book of hers too, not to mention the tin can she'd been so attached to. And once she'd forgotten them, it was as though they'd never even existed.

'That's the way it goes,' said Hirasaka. 'We have to let go of certain memories as we make our way through life.'

A short while later, he brought her a cup of tea on a tray and quietly set it down at her side. Alongside the steaming cup was a slice of yokan bean cake. Her favourite.

At first, she'd had her doubts about this business with the photos. But revisiting all these long-forgotten memories and selecting the ones that would adorn her lantern had come to seem like rather a charming final task in life.

She took a sip of the freshly brewed green tea, followed by a bite of the cake.

'Thank you. I always loved a bit of yokan.'

'I'm glad it's to your taste,' said Hirasaka, nodding contentedly.

'Are you sure you don't mind me taking so long?'

'Not in the slightest. Take as long as you need. And don't worry about me – I actually enjoy watching people spend time with their memories like this,' replied Hirasaka, taking a sip of tea.

Glancing sideways at him, Hatsue thought it was time

to ask another question. This time, it was Hirasaka himself she was curious about.

'Mr Hirasaka, I know you run this place, but are you . . . a human? Sorry, perhaps that's not a very polite way of putting it . . .'

Cupping his teacup in both hands, Hirasaka gave a self-effacing smile. 'Well, I'm certainly not a god or anything, if that's what you mean. I've been doing this job for a long time, but yes, I was once a human in the world of the living, just like you.'

His response surprised her. What kind of a life had he lived, she wondered? She couldn't quite picture him as a regular office worker. He was too calm and composed, somehow.

'Hmm, let me guess. Did you work in an art gallery, or a museum maybe? Or maybe a photo studio like this one?'

'No . . .'

'Well then, were you a company man? Whereabouts did you live? The way you speak makes me think Tokyo, or at least that neck of the woods . . .'

'Hmm . . .' said Hirasaka. The smile on his face was unchanged, but he seemed vaguely uneasy. Maybe she shouldn't have asked. In her old age, she had developed a bad habit of prying into other people's business.

She changed the subject in an attempt to break the

awkward silence. 'Ah, by the way, about these ones . . .' Her hand slipped, and several photos slid out from the pile on the corner of the desk and fell off the table, before splaying out in a colourful fan on the carpet.

'Oops!' Before she could reach down, Hirasaka quickly returned the photos to the desk.

On top of the pile was a photo of an old Tokyo bus.

'Ah, that old thing,' Hatsue found herself muttering. 'I remember it well . . .'

There were several other photos of the bus underneath, too. They must have caught Hirasaka's attention, because as he gathered the photos together he said: 'I see you liked buses. Did you work at a bus company or something?'

'No. In fact, my job had nothing to do with buses!'

'I see,' said Hirasaka. 'It's just there are all these photos of this one, so I thought it might be a clue!'

Hatsue gave a pensive sigh. 'Well, you could certainly say it played an important role in my life. And, technically, I did work *on* it for a while.' As she spoke, she reached for one of the photos of the bus.

'Oh dear. This one is . . .'

Of all her memories of the bus, there had been one she'd been looking forward to more than any other. But now that she'd finally found the photo in question, it was strangely washed out, making it hard to see the details. If she looked closely, she could just about make out the scene, but the image was bleached and faded. The bottom was the only part that was still properly visible, and appeared to show the legs of a crowd of people standing on a patch of muddy ground.

'Mr Hirasaka, look. I was really looking forward to this one, but it's all faded. You can barely see a thing!'

'Ah, my apologies. Where possible, the photos have been restored or corrected, but I'm afraid that particular one might have been beyond saving. Think about it this way: when you really treasure a photo, you put it on display or get it out and look at it all the time instead of simply storing it away – and as a result, those are the ones that end up faded and torn. Well, it's the same with memories. The more important a memory, the more we find ourselves revisiting it. But in doing so, the details can begin to evade us . . .'

'Is that so . . .' said Hatsue, disappointed. All she'd wanted was a glimpse. One last chance to take in that scene.

'This was a very important day for me and that bus,' she murmured, still gazing at the photo. 'I was twenty-three at the time, which would make it . . .'

'Nineteen forty-nine.' It seemed Hirasaka had already done the maths.

'Ah, thank you,' said Hatsue with a smile. 'Yes, I even

remember the date. It was the fourth of July . . .' She sank back into thought for a moment. 'Nineteen forty-nine, eh? That's a fair way back. I suppose it *was* about time I kicked the bucket, wasn't it . . .'

'Don't you worry,' said Hirasaka. He appeared to be making a note of the date Hatsue had mentioned. 'The photo might be faded, but there's a way we can restore it.'

'Restore it? What, do you have the negatives or something?'

'No, not here,' said Hirasaka.

How were they going to restore the photo if they had nothing to work with, she wondered?

Hirasaka took the faded photo in his hand, taking care not to touch the surface. 'If we returned to the exact time and place that this photo was taken, and took it again – well, we'd have a brand-new version of it, wouldn't we?'

'But . . . how?'

'It's possible for us to go back into the past – just for one day, mind – in order to retake the photo. And we can take whichever camera you'd like.'

Hirasaka got up and walked over to the door next to the one leading to the white room.

'This is the equipment room. Please – take a look.'

Hatsue gasped as she peered inside. As far as the eye could see, packed tightly on shelves that rose all the way to the ceiling, were hundreds and hundreds of cameras. She counted the shelves; there were ten of them. The top ones would be impossible to reach without a footstool. It was such an overwhelming sight that for a moment she was unable to move.

'Go on. Step inside,' said Hirasaka.

She walked in and looked around. The bottom shelves were filled with old, vaguely familiar-looking cameras – big wooden boxes with glinting brass tubes that must have been their lenses. The shelves above those were packed with a slightly more recent selection of classic cameras, some with not just one but two lenses protruding from their bodies. As her eyes passed from these to the shelf above, and then the shelf above that, she began to feel almost dizzy.

She had once read somewhere that when elephants die, they slip away from the herd and make their way to a sort of graveyard, home to the remains of other elephants from the herd, where they await their own death. This felt like the camera equivalent: a burial ground where all these devices had come to rest.

It was a truly staggering collection. There were even steps leading down to a lower level, where another enormous storage room awaited.

'We have every type of camera and lens here, from all over the world. That includes digital cameras and all the latest models. Please, feel free to use whichever you like.'

'It's . . . like a museum in here.'

'You'd be surprised how demanding people can be about the camera they take with them. They know it's the last photo they'll ever take, so they insist on a particular set-up,' said Hirasaka with a wry grin.

'But I don't even know where to start looking. I'm not much of a camera person, you see.'

Hatsue tried picking up one of the devices nearby, but it was some kind of professional digital camera, and she couldn't work out how to operate it. The body was heavier than it looked, and felt odd in her hands. She must have pushed a button somewhere, because it started making a *cha-cha-cha-cha* sound. Just as she began to panic, Hirasaka calmly relieved her of the camera, turned it off and returned it to the shelf.

'Now, I might be your guide, but I'm not allowed to take the photo for you. That's your job. But don't worry – you just tell me which cameras you like the look of, and we'll pick one out together. I promise we'll find one you feel comfortable with.'

Hatsue was relieved to hear this.

'We'll return to a day in the past,' he continued, 'although only to the time and place of the photograph you're recreating. Unfortunately, with you being a departed soul, and it being the past we're visiting, the people we encounter won't be able to see us. We won't be able to talk to or touch anyone. All we can do is go there, observe things, and take pictures.'

'So we just sort of . . . look around? I won't be able to talk to my parents, or anyone else we run into? How sad . . .' Hatsue glanced at the digital camera she'd picked up a moment ago. 'Modern cameras seem a bit fiddly. All those buttons and whatnot. I've never taken a photo this important before. I wonder if I'm really up to this . . .'

Hirasaka smiled reassuringly. 'To tell the truth, I was never much of a camera expert either. I've picked up quite a bit from the people who pass through here, though.'

'Funny, I thought it'd be the other way round!'

'Even in death, people love sharing their knowledge. Although I must say they can go on a bit sometimes.'

Hatsue laughed. 'I suppose some people never change, do they!'

'Exactly. But I'm grateful, really. I've learned a huge amount,' said Hirasaka, moving further into the equipment room. 'Now then, about that camera. How about this one?'

'Ah, yes,' said Hatsue. 'That does look familiar.'

She had definitely seen the camera somewhere before. She couldn't remember the exact name of the model, but she was fairly sure it was a Canon.

'Oh, good. I spotted it in some of the photos you were looking at, so I thought you might recognize it. It's a Canon Autoboy. How about trying to take a photo, if you remember how?'

She took the camera and tried pressing various buttons.

'I do remember it, but it's all a little hazy . . . You had to put film in it, didn't you . . .'

'Let me handle that part. Now, when you want to take a photo, this here is the shutter release,' said Hirasaka, pointing to the button in question. 'Try pressing it halfway down.'

Hatsue nodded.

'When you do that, the lens will automatically find focus,' explained Hirasaka. 'Those cameras take great photos. Apparently, back in the day, even the pros used them as their back-up. It hardly weighs a thing, and you can always be sure you'll get the shot. A solid choice, I'd say.'

Hatsue spent a few moments peering through the view-finder and getting a feel for the camera. Before long, she felt like she'd just about got the knack of it again.

'It *is* light. Perfect for time travelling!' said Hatsue.

Hirasaka nodded. 'I'm sure we'll have a wonderful trip.'

'I don't suppose you have a strap or something so I can hang it around my neck?'

Hirasaka opened a cupboard and began rooting around. 'Any particular colour you'd prefer?'

'How about blue?' she said.

Hirasaka fished out a sky-blue leather strap and handed it to her.

'We'll take plenty of film with us, so don't worry about messing up. When the time feels right, just snap away. We'll develop your best shot as a print. I'll show you how it all works in the darkroom, so you can let me know exactly how bright or colourful you want to make it.'

Hirasaka led her into the white room and stood in front of the door that appeared to lead outside.

'Right then. The fourth of July, nineteen forty-nine – from the first ray of sunrise until daybreak the following morning. All set with your camera?'

Standing at his side, Hatsue nodded.

'Then we're ready. Now, let's go find that bus of yours!'

Hirasaka opened the door.

———

All of a sudden, Hatsue felt the wind on her cheeks.

They were outside, walking along an embankment. Alarmed, Hatsue turned around, but the door they'd stepped through was nowhere to be seen.

In the distance, she could make out a familiar sight: the four distinctive smokestacks of the local power plant, known as the 'Ghost Chimneys' because they seemed to disappear or vary in number depending on your point of view. They had been demolished a long time ago, but back then they were visible for miles, a symbol of the Adachi ward of Tokyo. There were no tall apartment blocks in sight, and the roads were still unpaved. The embankment was simply a mound of earth, with none of the retaining walls that were built later. And instead of the massive bridge that now spanned the river, a ferryboat was making its way across the channel at a leisurely pace.

'Oh my. Everything really is just as it was,' said Hatsue.

'It's lovely,' said Hirasaka, also taking in their surroundings. An early-morning breeze was blowing.

'It always felt much cooler back then, maybe because everything wasn't paved over. The summers are sweltering these days, aren't they! You hear about people dying just because they forgot to put their air conditioning on . . .'

The sky, blue and cloudless, felt somehow more expansive – maybe because there were no tall buildings to get in the way.

'The air feels purer somehow, too. And look how clean the river used to be.'

'Well, we've plenty of time. How about a walk?' said Hirasaka.

They began ambling along the riverside.

'I suppose I could tell you some stories from back then,' said Hatsue. 'But I wouldn't know where to start. And I don't imagine you'd be very interested in the ramblings of an old fogie like me . . .'

'Not at all – please, tell me anything you like. I'm very interested in the life you led here.'

'I suppose you're the last person I'll ever be able to chat to like this, aren't you?'

'Yes, I suppose I am.'

And so, with her eyes fixed on the embankment that stretched ahead of them, Hatsue began her story.

It was the story of a small neighbourhood in Adachi, Tokyo, and it began the year before their arrival, in nineteen forty-eight.

———— • ————

I raced down the embankment, threw off my smock and shoes, and plunged into the river.

The icy water was like a vice around my heart, but there was no time for second thoughts. I'd always been good at swimming, if not much else. I thrust my arms forward and, still riding the momentum from my dive, began pulling myself along. The water stung as it rushed up my nose, but I kept kicking, gliding for as long as my lungs would allow. When, eventually, my mouth broke the surface, I took in a lungful of air and carried on propelling myself through the water, every stroke faster and stronger than the last.

With all the rainfall in the last few days, the current was stronger than usual, and I was beginning to feel its pull. Still, knowing I needed to close the distance, I aligned my forehead with my target and focused on my kick.

It was my middle finger that made contact first. Then, as the current carried me along, I managed to grasp what felt like a collar.

'Hey, hang in there!'

I tried to pull the little boy above the water, but he was cold and limp in my arms. At least he didn't weigh too much. Floating on my back and holding him by the armpits, I swam sidestroke back towards the shore.

Glancing over, I saw that some passers-by on the embankment had finally noticed what was happening. One after the other, they began diving in and making their way towards me.

Eventually, someone threw me a rope. I grabbed hold of it and was yanked ashore.

The boy I'd pulled from the water must have been only three or four years old. His bare feet were pale and drained of colour. He wasn't breathing.

'Someone's gone for a doctor.'

'I know some CPR.' It was a skill I'd only just learned. I'd hardly expected to end up using it so soon.

Breathing as hard as I could into the boy's mouth, I saw his chest rise slightly. It was a pitiful little movement. I placed one hand on top of the other where his heart would be and, using my body weight, began pumping away.

One, two, three, one, two, three . . .

From the crowd behind me I heard people muttering.

Who is she? – She's got guts, hasn't she – Diving in like that . . .

I pushed down firmly on the boy's stomach. With a sudden heave, he began coughing up water. After a few feeble breaths, he began to cry. His mother, who had just dashed over, her hair a mess, now hugged him close as she too burst into tears. I was just getting my breath back when I spotted them in the crowd. The other children.

When our eyes met, they hurriedly looked away. But I wasn't going to let them off the hook.

'*You lot!*' I shouted. 'Playing by the river all on your own, on a day like this – what were you thinking?!'

They hung their heads in shame. It was true that the river-bank was the perfect spot for kite-flying or, in the summer, catching dragonflies or diving beetles in the ponds. But today the river was swollen with rainwater. They would have been told over and over again never to go near it on days like this.

Someone told me to calm down, but I wasn't listening.

'He followed me down to the river,' said one of the children. 'Even though I told him to wait at the top of the bank.'

'That's right,' chimed in another. 'We were just wondering where he'd gone, and then all of sudden we realized he'd fallen in over there.'

I'd only been walking along the river because I'd been offered a job nearby and had wanted to see what the area was like. Then I'd spotted something moving in the murky water. I dreaded to think what would have happened if I hadn't.

'Never *ever* play on your own here when it's been raining. Okay?'

The children began mumbling in response.

'What's that? Speak up!'

'Yes, miss!'

One of the younger children pointed at my nose.

'Miss, your nose is running.'

Flustered, I wiped the snot away with my right hand.

Before all this had happened, I'd had my doubts about taking on the job. It was a lengthy commute from where I lived, and the pay didn't seem worth it. I'd have to change trains and cross a rickety old bridge just to get here, and the building itself was far from ideal. People in my profession were in high demand these days, so I was sure I'd be able to find somewhere more pleasant to work.

I sneezed loudly, and felt my nose about to run again. A woman from the crowd handed me some dry clothes and told me I could wear them. She kept bowing to me.

Finally, the local policeman came running over.

'Thank you for saving the boy's life. Can I get your name and age?'

'Hatsue Mishima. Twenty-three.'

'Very brave of you jumping in like that, miss. The river is rough today.'

'Well, children are worth whatever it takes,' I said, looking the policeman in the eyes.

He nodded deeply. 'Do you live around here?'

'No.'

'Then you're here for work?'

'That's right.'

The police officer looked at me as if to ask: *And what work is that?*

'I'm a nursery teacher.'

'Sorry?'

'A nursery teacher! I only start the day after tomorrow, though.'

I sneezed, even louder this time, and my nose started running again. The policeman offered me a handkerchief.

It was so windy that day that the smoke from the Ghost Chimneys was blowing horizontally. I had made my decision: I would stay and work as a nursery teacher here in Aratano.

———

Unlike my own neighbourhood on the outskirts of Toshima, which had escaped the worst of the air raids, the heavily industrialized Aratano area had been relentlessly targeted. In fact, the entire neighbourhood, which lay within the curve of the river, had been practically razed to the ground.

Even now that the war was over, the authorities, anxious to boost reconstruction efforts, had prioritized the rebuilding of factories over housing. But of course, factories need a workforce, and so Aratano's population had grown rapidly in turn. With more and more families moving to the area, each with children to feed, everyone was struggling just to get by.

In those chaotic post-war years, many jobs had simply ceased to exist, and unemployment was widespread. Even those lucky enough to remain in employment often received their wages late. And because those wages were the only thing keeping them going, things could quickly turn desperate. Even mothers with small children had to leave their young children unattended and take on piecework or even full-time jobs in order to put food on the table.

Soon it became common for the oldest child to look after their younger siblings during the day. But, kids being kids, they ended up in all sorts of danger – smacking their heads on this or that, getting hit by cars or, like today, almost drowning themselves in the river.

Some of the parents banded together and set up improvised daycare centres, with different parents looking after the children depending on the day of the week. But that was hardly a viable long-term solution, and naturally there was a huge demand for professional nursery teachers.

Meanwhile, I had just passed my nursery teacher's exam. The Democratic League for Childcare had found me a job in Aratano, where a local steel company had offered a room to serve as a temporary nursery school.

The commute involved taking a tram from Toshima, then walking from the nearest station – a ninety-minute slog each way, all told. When I looked at the neighbourhood on a map, I saw that it was located on a sort of sandbar within the curve of the river, and as there were no bridges nearby, the fastest way of getting there would be by ferryboat.

But if I refused the job, they'd have to start looking for another nursery teacher who met the requirements, meaning it would be even longer until the nursery was up and running. In the meantime, more mothers would be forced to leave their children at home in order to work. Today, one of those children had almost drowned. I could barely imagine how distressing it must be to worry about your children drowning or injuring themselves while you were forced to work.

It certainly felt like fate that I'd got caught up in the

events at the river. But even more than that, I was an optimistic person by nature. Things would work out somehow, I told myself. On my way home, I posted a letter saying I'd take the job.

Still, I did wonder why, as a rookie who'd only just passed her exam, I'd been offered a job so quickly. It turned out there was a reason.

———

The early-morning light was dazzling. The clickety-clack of the tram was lulling me to sleep, but somehow I kept my drooping eyelids open. As the tram slowed, I glanced out of the window and saw that we were about to arrive at Kamiyabashi station.

Following the stream of people getting off the tram, I made my way along Koshin-dori. Boys on bicycles weaved effortlessly through the crowd. In front of me walked a young mother, her baby strapped to her back. The baby was staring in open-mouthed fascination at the signposts jutting up from the pavement, on each of which a different name had been written in huge characters. They were the names of the candidates for the recently held elections.

The pavement, if you could call it that, consisted of a series of concrete blocks, covered here and there with a thin layer of earth. I stepped carefully from block to block, squinting whenever the wind blew up a cloud of dust.

I glanced towards a passing taxi, but turned away when I saw that the starting fare was eighty yen – an astronomical figure for me at the time. I strode towards Aratano Bridge as fast as I could. It was a ramshackle old wooden structure whose planks audibly creaked as I crossed it. Through the gaps I could see the rushing river below.

The temporary nursery was in the vacant room the Democratic League for Childcare had managed to rent from the steel company. It was an unfurnished wooden-floored space on the first floor of the east wing of the company premises, just about wide enough for all the children, standing shoulder to shoulder, to form a circle. The complete absence of any teaching tools or other equipment wasn't ideal, but I planned to work around that.

In fact, I soon learned that the children would come up with plenty of ideas on their own. It was breathtaking to watch: a simple furoshiki cloth could become an ocean, or a rainstorm, or a house. Above all, I loved watching the children growing and learning day by day. Not just getting physically bigger, but learning to do things they'd never have managed just a few days before – changing at a speed that was unimaginable for adults. With just myself and one other teacher to look after thirty-two children, we were swept off our feet at times, but even so, it was always an enriching experience. I tried to pick up on each child's special talents and did everything I could to ensure they'd go home feeling like they'd had a good day.

We arranged to borrow a corner of the company grounds to use as an outdoor play area on sunny days. When we got out the big skipping rope, one of the kids would say, 'I don't want to, it's scary.' Then the others would all chime in with different, conflicting bits of advice: 'You jump when the rope's *here*!', 'No, you jump when it's *here*!' Still others would proudly declare they were the best at spinning the rope. All that fun, from a single length of rope!

'Alright then, we'll swing it nice and slow,' I'd say, and they'd all squeal with delight.

Make it go really high, Miss Mishima! Nice and slow!

There was barely enough money to keep the place going, and all we could give the children by way of snacks was a single hard candy each. And yet snack time still triggered whoops of excitement.

———

The problem started with the notes.

Wedged into the door of the classroom was a piece of paper with two words on it: *Shut up!* They were written in an elegant script that jarred with the blunt message. Baffled, I decided to ignore it, thinking it might have been a prank by one of the children.

But the next day, there was another note wedged into

the door, with the exact same message traced on it. Again, the characters wouldn't have looked out of place in a calligraphy contest, and yet somehow they seethed with anger. The final exclamation mark seemed almost to jump off the page with fury.

When I told someone at the steel company about the notes, they replied: 'Ah. That must be the lady who lives opposite the nursery.' From the way they spoke, it sounded like this 'lady' was a bit of a tough customer. Knowing that even a single sheet of paper was a valuable commodity in those days, I carefully smoothed the wrinkles out so that we'd get more for it at the next scrap paper collection.

The children didn't make *that* much noise when they were playing, and certainly not enough to warrant a message like that. We did sing the occasional song, but it wasn't like we had a piano or anything. The complaint seemed completely unreasonable.

Anyway, if we were so noisy, why didn't she just come and tell us to 'shut up' in person? There was only one home within earshot of the nursery, so it wasn't like she could have hoped to remain anonymous. No, the fact that she'd gone to the trouble of writing notes could only mean one thing: she was really quite furious.

Before long, she started complaining directly to the company that was leasing us the room.

Asking around, I managed to glean that the woman

who lived opposite the nursery was a young and somewhat volatile housewife. Her husband was a local magnate, and the family had lived there for a very long time. One day, I decided to leave the children in the care of the other teacher and visit her to apologize about the noise. Surely if I explained things face to face she'd understand.

As I said, the entire area had been firebombed to the ground during the war, and yet the grand old house in question, with its earthen walls, had escaped the flames. By the gated entrance rose a magnificent if slightly crooked pine tree, alongside a plate bearing the name *Hisano*.

'Hello?' I called from the entrance. An old woman emerged who seemed to be the maid.

'My name is Hatsue Mishima. I teach at the nursery opposite. I'm very sorry to impose, but could I possibly speak to the lady of the house?'

'Just a moment, please,' said the maid, and disappeared – before reappearing almost immediately with a composed expression. 'Mrs Hisano can't see you right now.'

'I came to apologize. It seems we've been making too much noise,' I explained. The maid withdrew again, before quickly returning.

'The lady says you're to stop the racket immediately.'

Given how quickly the maid kept re-emerging, Mrs Hisano must have been sitting in a room right next to the entrance. I felt my hands and feet growing cold as the

43

blood rushed to my head. What on earth was the point of this game of pass-it-on? There were times when people needed to look each other in the face and talk, and this was one of them.

'Excuse me!' I yelled into the house, clasping my hands behind my back and sticking my chest out slightly to make my voice project. 'It's me, from the nursery school! I'm very sorry for all the noise!'

When Mrs Hisano finally appeared in the doorway, she was all dressed up in fancy Western clothes. She looked rather fragile – no wonder she had such delicate nerves, I found myself thinking. She was beautiful, but something about her also reminded me of a spool of tightly wound thread. She studied me from head to toe as if making some kind of assessment. Once her gaze had arrived at my feet, it returned to my face, after which a lengthy silence ensued. Then, just as I was about to start my apology, she suddenly exploded.

'Noise?! It's an *abominable* racket!'

We locked eyes. The maid hovered helplessly at one side, her eyes darting nervously between the two of us.

'I'm sorry the children's voices bother you so much.'

'I can barely hear myself think! My nerves are in tatters!'

'We'll do our best to keep the noise to a minimum, so please bear with us. Listen, I'm sorry to say this, but children do need nurturing *somewhere*.'

'Nurturing,' said Mrs Hisano, before falling silent for a moment. 'That's what you're doing, is it? Nurturing them?'

'That's right. Children are the future, aren't they? And our job as nursery school teachers is to help them develop into healthy young people. Every day they grow a little bit more, and by playing with toys and engaging in group activities, that growth can be—'

'You're not married, are you?' she interrupted.

'No, I'm not.'

'You can talk about *nurturing* them all you like, but you're really just a glorified babysitter, aren't you?'

I felt the blood rising to my cheeks. So I was unmarried – what difference did that make?

'You don't even have children,' she went on. 'What on earth do you know?' She had probably been mentally rehearsing this tirade every day as she stared in the direction of the nursery.

'Just make it stop, you hear? That's all I have to say to you.' As I was about to leave, she added: 'Also, I can't *bear* that song of yours. You're always a half-tone out at the end.'

On the way back to the nursery, I bumped into the children, who had just been out for a walk along the embankment. They came running over, shouting, 'Miss Mishima!'

I managed a smile. 'What insects did you find on the embankment, then?'

'Grasshoppers! Ladybirds!' they shouted back. Worrying about their loud voices, I glanced at Mrs Hisano's house just in time to see the window slam shut.

After that, I made sure to steer well clear of the house whenever we went outside. I kept the windows of the nursery closed, and whenever the children got too noisy I'd get them to play quietly with toys or draw.

But it seemed that wasn't enough. Not long afterwards, the steel company told us they could no longer provide the room. They didn't give us a detailed explanation, but it seemed someone had forced their hand.

I couldn't quite believe it. We were told to clear everything out and vacate the premises by the start of the following week. The real panic was among the parents. There were no other suitable buildings for a nursery school in the area. If we couldn't find somewhere to look after the children, the situation would become unsustainable. Mrs Sakaida, a senior member of the parent–teacher association, summoned the parents for an emergency meeting. She always liked to take charge of these meetings, but with a solution seemingly out of reach she became increasingly shrill.

Eventually, it was decided that, for the time being, we'd look after the children on the embankment. On rainy days, we'd arrange to borrow a room at one of the parents' houses.

———

Rain was leaking through my battered umbrella as I made my way home. I had to hold it at a precise angle to avoid the drips.

Not only was the Aratano neighbourhood almost encircled by a river, but the land itself was also low-lying. Whenever it rained, huge puddles would form and the rudimentary roads would turn treacherous and muddy. My shoes would get filthy, and I'd have to wash them as soon as I got home. No matter how carefully I walked, my clothes always ended up spattered with mud too.

By the time I finally reached the narrow street where I lived, it was pitch dark. I opened the badly fitted door, folded up my umbrella and put my shoes in the washtub. I was famished. My younger siblings were already fast asleep.

'You can't keep coming home this late, Hatsue,' said my mother, serving me a huge pile of rice. Sitting upright at the low table, I joined my hands together to say thank you, then tucked in. A small bowl of pickles was shoved in my direction.

'I wish you'd give this nursery thing up,' she continued. 'It's not worth what you're putting yourself through. Next

47

week you might not even have a roof over your head, never mind a school! It's ridiculous . . .'

The other nursery teacher had recently decided to quit, for precisely this reason.

'But if I quit now, what will the children do?'

'Oh, they'll manage somehow. Kids always do.'

'But they need proper childcare to—'

'That's not for you to worry about! It's just a job, Hatsue!'

'But—'

'No buts. They haven't even paid you this month, have they?'

This was true. My salary was only paid in instalments, and even those were often delayed for weeks at a time. This time, it had been three weeks and counting.

'Why don't you get a job that pays you on time? There must be plenty of better-equipped nurseries out there. I mean, really – looking after children on a riverbank, of all places . . .'

It's not worth what you're putting yourself through. This was one of mother's favourite lines.

Every day, I got home after dark, ate supper, prepared the following day's activities, and collapsed straight into bed, but I never seemed to sleep very well.

You're just a glorified babysitter, aren't you?

Given the conditions I was working in, it was hardly

surprising Mrs Hisano's words had lingered in my mind. I'd always prided myself on doing my best, as a nursery teacher, to ensure the children were always safe and able to learn and grow. But our nursery school was a makeshift affair: the premises were temporary, and everything from the organizational structure to the pay system had been hastily improvised. The other teacher, who had also been in charge of the accounts, had already quit, leaving me solely responsible for the children.

Right now, fewer than half the parents were paying their fees regularly. When they told me it had been a tough month and bowed their heads in apology, I felt like there was nothing I could say. Since starting the job, there hadn't been a single day when I'd got home before dark. I was still new to the job, and the organization itself had only recently been formed, so perhaps I couldn't complain. But going for half a month without a salary wasn't easy. I kept telling myself I should at least get a new umbrella – and yet here I was, with the same old battered one.

Sometimes the parents wouldn't even turn up to collect their child at the end of the day. I couldn't exactly leave them there and eat dinner on my own, so I'd often end up splitting a steamed bun or something with the child in question. I had to cover those sorts of unexpected expenses out of pocket, and soon I was spending large amounts of my own money. I could hardly issue an invoice for half a steamed bun.

All that kept me going was the pride I took in being a nursery teacher. But what if the parents themselves thought of me only as a 'glorified babysitter'? What if they assumed they were simply paying someone to look after their children, rather than raise them on their behalf?

I could feel my initial determination beginning to waver. How long could I keep this up?

———

It was our last day at the steel company's premises. I was getting on with some paperwork while glancing frequently out of the window. I knew that on that particular day of the week, Mrs Hisano always walked out into the street in order to hail a taxi.

When I spotted her, I asked the other teacher to watch the children, then went out and approached her. She backed away from me slightly, clutching her bag to her chest, as though afraid of being confronted by me. The Hisano family owned the land that the company's offices were on, and I was convinced she'd had a hand in the nursery's closure.

'Well, thank you for putting up with us, but it seems we're leaving.' I said, bowing my head. 'I apologize for all the inconvenience our noise must have caused you.'

A moment ago, she'd been looking at me like she thought I was about to stab her. My apology seemed to have caught her off guard.

'But one day, I'm going to build a wonderful nursery here in Aratano.' She stared at me. 'The kind of nursery where even *you* would be happy to send your children.' I bowed again. She still hadn't said a word.

'Well, I must be going,' I said, and left her standing there.

Back at the nursery, playtime was in full swing. Some of the kids were playing house, while others were amusing themselves with spinning tops.

I noticed a piece of paper on my desk. On it were the words 'Miss Mishima', together with a portrait of me with big round eyes. The drawing had been done with a pencil, and the grain of the desk showed through the strokes. A few wobbly lines aside, they'd done a pretty good job of capturing my round face, nose and eyes. They'd even decorated the area around the face with drawings of yokan bean cake, my favourite.

You've got this, I told myself.

———

It looked like it was going to be a hot day. I crossed the Aratano Bridge, climbed the embankment, and made my way over to the open field, watching the reeds sway in the wind as I walked. In my hands, sweating from the long journey, I was holding the storytelling cards that the children loved so much.

They must have spotted me walking along the embankment, because they soon came bounding over with their usual excited cries of 'Miss Mishima!'

First, we all held hands and walked along the embankment. When the time was right, we sat in a circle and began singing a song, with me providing the melody on a harmonica.

'Into the hat goes a . . . tomato!'

The children took turns replacing the word 'tomato' with their favourite fruit, each time triggering a chorus of giggles. When it was my turn, I shouted 'yokan' instead.

Afterwards, we ran around catching insects, playing with the leaves and making flower wreaths. Their cheerful voices seemed to fill the clear blue sky.

Still, with no one else to help, keeping an eye on all the children playing on the embankment was a serious challenge. With concerns about their safety mounting, a parents' meeting was held, and it was decided that any mothers and fathers who could spare the time would help look after the children.

Whenever I talked to the parents, we always agreed on the need for a proper nursery. It didn't matter if the building was temporary or borrowed; all we wanted was somewhere the children could be safe and dry. But these were the days of post-war reconstruction, and we weren't the only ones struggling. With the new yen having been issued, inflation was sky-high, and there was a shortage of timber and other construction materials. When timber *was* available, it was for absurdly high prices on the black market.

I'd proudly told Mrs Hisano that we'd have our own building one day, but I knew better than anyone what a fantasy that was. Ours was a small school, one the state hadn't even approved yet – and I still wasn't even being paid on time.

With the arrival of the rainy season, I could no longer take the children to the embankment. Instead, day after day, we borrowed a room in somebody's house.

The room would be packed so full of children that it was a struggle just to walk from one end to the other. As I looked around the crowded space, I told myself that we just needed to hold on a little longer. Someday, we would manage to rent a space. I didn't know when that day would come, or how long I'd be able to cope like this. All I could do was try to get through each day.

It was only later that I found out that Mrs Hisano had herself been continually berated by her mother-in-law for failing to bear children.

You don't even have children. What on earth do you know?

Her words that day had cut me like a knife, but now I realized they were only the expression of a pain she herself had felt for years.

———

It was a gloomy day in the rainy season. Grey skies overhead and warm, muggy air that seemed to cling to your skin. An unsettled wind had been blowing since the morning. Rain was forecast for the afternoon, and as usual we had relocated to the house where I was looking after the children.

Watching them playing with dolls on the floor, I noticed that some of them seemed a little sluggish.

'Miss, I'm sleepy,' said one of the children. I put a hand to her forehead; she had a temperature. Some of the other children said they were feeling unwell too. Must be a cold going around, I thought to myself.

One mother who had come to pick up her child said: 'I wonder if it's some kind of stomach bug?' I'd begun thinking the same thing. But the reality turned out to be much worse.

Just after we'd seen everyone off for the day, the woman whose house we'd been borrowing came rushing over. Her face was pale. We learned that the grandfather of the house had recently fallen ill, and today had gone to the hospital for an examination, where he'd been diagnosed with dysentery. Now that I thought about it, we hadn't seen him for a couple of days.

Then it hit me. The children had been using the same toilet as the old man.

Dysentery begins with a fever, followed by severe stomach pain, diarrhoea and bloody stools. The symptoms last for days, and the disease is highly contagious. In young children in particular, it can result in severe illness and often death – and once it occurs among a group of children, the infection can spread dramatically. In those days, there was no real treatment available.

Fearing the disease was the reason for the children's fever, I said a rushed goodbye and dashed off. I summoned the senior members of the parent–teacher association and asked them to contact all the other parents.

Seven children had been infected. Their parents rushed along the embankment towards the hospital, their children groaning feebly in their arms; I followed them.

Of the seven, two boys in the senior group had the most severe symptoms. Their condition was so bad that we couldn't take our eyes off them for a moment. Word reached us that even more of the children were falling ill.

'I'm so sorry,' I said, prostrating myself on the cold hospital floor in apology. Even when the parents told me they didn't blame me, I couldn't bring myself to stand up.

When I realized that some of the children might die,

I began wishing desperately that it had been an adult like me who had been infected instead.

Ten more children were admitted to the hospital the following morning, arriving in three groups, with two more joining them the next day. A total of nineteen children ended up in hospital – more than half the entire number at the nursery school. This was becoming a major incident.

When I heard that the two boys who had been in critical condition were out of danger, I was so relieved I practically collapsed in my chair. Still, the incubation period for dysentery was five days. I myself had no symptoms, but what if some of the younger children, with their weaker immune systems, had been infected?

I was scared to death. All I could do was pray.

During the day, I helped carry out a thorough disinfection of the home we'd been using as a nursery school, as well as those of all the patients. Stool samples were also collected from the relevant families. The health centre and the neighbourhood association helped put a support system in place.

In between disinfecting the houses, helping out at the hospital, and visiting the sick children, I barely had time to go home.

Various parents told me I looked exhausted and should get some rest, but this was no time to be sitting around at home. After all, there was every possibility that one of my pupils might die.

Eventually, we realized that only the children who had used the toilet in the house had dysentery. One small mercy was that the junior group were still using potties rather than going to the bathroom.

For the entire month that the children were in hospital, the nursery stopped running. Patients with dysentery were kept in an isolation ward, which meant that even family members were prevented from visiting freely. During their isolation, we brought them letters and toys every day.

Apparently, the children were behaving very responsibly during their stay, and those who were past the worst of their illness had even decided on their own duty rota. The hospital staff praised them for having a cleaner ward than the adult patients.

One day, I was just heading home when someone handed me a letter, carefully folded in four. Apparently it was from the children.

Dear Miss Mishima. It'll be dark on the way home, so watch out for cars, okay?

Next to the message were lots of drawings of yokan.

Unable to hold back my tears, I dabbed at my eyes with my sleeve.

Dysentery claimed more than twenty thousand lives in

the period following the war. But, by some miracle, every one of my pupils survived.

———

Just as the nursery was about to reopen, I was informed that Mr and Mrs Sakaida had convened all the parents for another emergency meeting. My heart was heavy as I made my way to the community centre where the meeting was to be held. After the drama of the dysentery outbreak, I was sure the discussion wasn't going to be a pleasant one.

Despite my supposedly neutral status as teacher, I couldn't help but prefer some parents over others. While I was careful never to let my feelings show, I'd always found the Sakaidas particularly hard to handle.

With her well-built frame, Mrs Sakaida tended to dominate proceedings much more than her diminutive husband. The head of a successful advertising business, she was one of the most influential businesspeople in the Aratano area. Like some flamboyant tropical bird, she never stopped moving and talking. She enjoyed spouting pseudo-intellectual phrases, and invariably brought up some pearl of educational wisdom that she'd picked up at the all-girls' school she'd attended; in short, she could be quite annoying. She also seemed convinced that I was some weak-kneed rookie in desperate need of her expert guidance.

She had already started drilling her own children in reading and writing, and she never missed a chance to suggest that we study the Analects of Confucius at the nursery. When I explained that I believed children should first learn about the world through play, with textbooks only coming later, she would smirk and reply: 'Oh, so you're a devotee of the Montessori method.' It was all quite exasperating.

The parents were sitting in tightly packed rows. I made my way to the front and bowed deeply, scarcely able to breathe.

So this was it, I thought – I was going to be publicly denounced for my actions. If only I could have watched over the children for a while longer – at least until my current group had moved up to primary school.

Their faces came to mind, one after the other. Mari, who had recently mastered the skipping rope. Takeru, so proud of his somersaults on the horizontal bars. And little Ren, the expert at drawing trains.

Then I realized that every single parent in the room was staring intently at me, and I almost stopped breathing altogether.

'Everyone, I am very sorry for the trouble I've caused. Although the children have all recovered, I would like to apologize sincerely for allowing this distressing situation to occur.'

The room was deathly silent. I was afraid to raise my deeply bowed head.

'Oh, there's no need for that, Miss Mishima,' said Mrs Sakaida. 'We all appreciate your hard work. However, that is not the reason for today's meeting.' She paused. 'Now then, everyone, I'd like you to think about something. How would you feel if one thousand yen disappeared from the wallet of every person here?'

The listening parents remained silent, their troubled faces suggesting they didn't quite know where Mrs Sakaida was going with this. I didn't either.

Mrs Sakaida looked around the room, then nodded. 'You'd be angry, wouldn't you? Of course you would. It'd be stealing.'

Had there been some kind of theft in the wake of the dysentery outbreak? I began to panic.

'And what if that was exactly what someone in this very room was going through?'

Nobody said a word. Then she turned to me.

'Miss Mishima.'

'Y-yes?' I croaked, barely able to speak.

'I'm told you still haven't been paid for some of May and the whole of June. Is that true?'

'Erm . . . yes.' I was so flustered I was barely even aware of what I was saying. 'But people can, erm, pay when they have the money. There's no rush.'

'Miss Mishima.' Her tone was icy. And here came that terrifying stare of hers. 'Perhaps you've misunderstood.'

'Misunderstood? No, really, about my salary, it's fine . . .'

'Listen. You haven't been given the money you're owed. That's the same as someone taking it out of your purse. It's exploitation of labour. Exploitation!'

By now I'd broken out in a sweat. It took me a moment to connect the sound of the word *exploitation* with its meaning.

'Exploitation? Oh, no . . . I mean, I'm just happy to be learning and growing along with the children . . .'

'Think of a fishmonger, or a tofu shop. They give you food, you pay them money – that's how it works. Why should childcare be any different? Shouldn't people pay for that too?'

'I know, but . . . well, a lot of families are really struggling these days.'

'Yes, some households may simply not have the means to pay. But this really is an alarming situation. We might not have a proper nursery school, but we can at least pay the teacher who looks after our children for us! Otherwise, can we really claim, in good conscience, that we're responsible parents?'

'Oh no,' I said, overwhelmed by Mrs Sakaida's onslaught. 'Really, I don't mind . . .'

'Come on, think about this properly,' she said, her tone

even sharper now. 'Even if you really don't mind, think about the teachers who'll come after you. Yes, it is very, *very* important that teachers feel motivated. But if they use that motivation as a pretext for letting themselves be exploited, how will they ever inspire the next generation of teachers? When you're being treated like that, can you really go around proudly telling people that childcare is a job for highly skilled professionals?'

By now the room was so quiet you could hear a pin drop.

'I want everyone to make sure they're always on time with their fees, whatever the circumstances. Now, there's one more thing.'

There was a loud thud as Mrs Sakaida stamped her foot. 'We *need* our own nursery!'

The parents began murmuring pessimistically among themselves.

But we can't afford it.

There's no money to pay for it.

With everyone struggling to make ends meet, it was hardly realistic to expect them to donate money for a new nursery school.

'Everyone, I'd like to present my fundraising plan!'

Mrs Sakaida dramatically unfurled a rolled-up piece of paper. On it were scrawled the words: *Beer Hall and Night Market Fundraising Plan.*

'You might not have any money, but you can still chip in. In other words, even if they can't donate, how about every family provides as much physical assistance as they can? Any unwanted possessions can be donated to the jumble sale. So please, everyone. Let's make this happen!'

There were even more murmurs.

It's tough for everyone these days.

We don't have time for this kind of thing!

'Quiet, please!' shouted Mrs Sakaida. 'Tell me, are we really going to let our children run around in the open, without a nursery of their own? Shouldn't we at least provide them with shelter from the wind and rain? We need to think of what's best for them!' She abruptly turned to me. 'Isn't that right, Miss Mishima?'

'Oh, erm, yes. If we can organize an event like you suggest, I'll do my best to help. I believe children are worth whatever it takes, and hopefully this is one way we can help them. I just want them to have somewhere nice to play.'

There was a sprinkling of applause. It grew until, suddenly, everyone was clapping their hands. I stood there with my head lowered.

As everyone was leaving, I walked up to Mrs Sakaida.

'Thank you. That was, erm, very kind of you.'

'Oh, that wasn't about helping you. I just think money that's owed ought to be paid! It's basic economics.'

63

She really is hard as nails, I thought to myself. But still, I was glowing inside.

'Besides, there's no guarantee the plan will work.' Mrs Sakaida looked at me. 'Still, sometimes you have to take a gamble. Can't just sit around twiddling our thumbs, can we!'

And with that, she walked off.

After that, my salary was almost always paid on time. Miraculously enough, it even went up slightly. Soon I managed to replace my battered old umbrella.

That meeting might have changed how the parents viewed the nursery, but it also made me see my job in a whole new light.

———

With lights illuminating the grounds of the local shrine, a real festival atmosphere had set in. A queue had formed in front of the ice-cream stand, with the boy at the front asking for an extra big scoop. The lid was lifted from the large, round container to reveal its glistening contents, the colour of egg yolk. A man wearing a headband was pulling up the ice cream with a round scoop and moulding it onto the cones.

'Careful you don't drop it, now!' he called. Noticing me, he smiled. 'Fancy a scoop, Miss Mishima? Go on, treat yourself!' He was one of the numerous locals who had decided to help us in our mission to secure a building for the nursery.

Nearby, pork was sizzling away on a griddle, filling the air with a mouth-watering aroma. The group of fathers running the stand skilfully added cabbage to the pan, then began stir-frying the lot. Drawn by the smoke, a few children had gathered in front of the griddle, where they waited impatiently. With the addition of noodles, a sprinkling of green laver and a squirt of sauce, the portion of yakisoba was ready for consumption – by which point a long, snaking queue had formed. Not far away, at the jumble sale, a group of mothers were selling various hand-sewn items of children's clothing.

The summer night filled with shouts of 'Yakitori! Freshly grilled yakitori!' and 'Beer! Ice-cold beer!' More and more people from the neighbourhood gathered under the lights, raising their drinks to one another. Nearby, children were drawing lots for a chance to win rice crackers. And, as the evening wore on, donation after donation landed in the collection box in the corner.

———

The night market had been a roaring success, but the money raised was still nowhere near enough to build a new nursery. Timber was still in short supply, and sourcing it on the black market would have been astronomically costly. We barely had enough to build an entrance, never mind a whole school. And we had no leads when it came to the most expensive part of all – buying a plot of land to build on.

———•———

By this point, Hirasaka and Hatsue were sitting on a bench in a small park. Around them, the cicadas were chirring away. When one of them started, the others would all join in. They lived such short lives, thought Hatsue – waiting patiently underground, briefly emerging into the world, then dying before they ever got to see another summer. Of course, they themselves were oblivious to all that. Gazing down at her hands, Hatsue looked back on her life and thought to herself that maybe humans weren't so different.

Hirasaka, meanwhile, seemed eager to hear the rest of her story.

'So you couldn't afford to build a new nursery?'

'There's only so much money you can raise from a single festival. And timber prices were through the roof back then. We had no choice but to abandon the plan.'

Hirasaka's face fell. 'Oh dear. What a shame!'

'But that wasn't the end of it . . .' said Hatsue, getting to her feet. The camera was dangling from her neck. 'I think it's almost time. Come on, up you get.'

A warm breeze was blowing across the embankment, despite the grey clouds that were gathering overhead. Shading her eyes with her hand, Hatsue gazed intently into the distance.

'Here it comes! Look, over there!'

First they heard the shouts: *Heave, heave!* Then the taiko drums: *don-don-don!* Mingled with these sounds were the excited voices of children.

A group of people tugging a rope came into view. At first, Hirasaka assumed they were pulling one of the massive floats usually seen at festivals. But no: the crowd was towing a large bus.

Mothers, some with children strapped to their backs, others in smocks with the sleeves rolled up; fathers in the long white cotton shorts usually worn at festivals – all sorts of people, dressed however they fancied, tugging as hard as they could on the thick ropes. Some of the older children were pulling too, while the younger ones cheered them on from the sides.

One particular group of women were leaning forward at an angle to the ground, their faces red with exertion.

'Look, that's me over there! My face is all purple. Gritting my teeth like that – I look like a dried plum!'

The taiko drums were louder now. *Don-don-don!*

'We couldn't afford our own building, but we did raise enough to buy an old bus that the Tokyo Transport

Authority was selling off. Then we managed to rent an unused patch of land at the bottom of the embankment.'

All of a sudden, a blanket of thick, dark cloud covered the sky, and heavy drops of rain began thudding into the ground. A squall was blowing in. Even the ghostly Hatsue, watching the bus from a distance, felt the rain. It wouldn't do for the camera to get wet, she thought, and slipped it into her pocket.

Then, as quickly as it had started, the rain seemed to stop: Hirasaka had smoothly opened up a folding umbrella and was sheltering her with it. How peculiar, she thought, to be sharing an umbrella at the end of my life with this strapping young man . . .

'The bus was basically ready for the scrap heap, so we weren't too surprised when the engine broke down on the way. We really ought to have had it towed, but we didn't have the money for that. We had to take a more . . . manual approach.'

Raindrops drummed noisily against the umbrella.

'Miss Mishima!' someone shouted. 'What should we do?'

'We're almost there!' came the assertive reply. 'Just a little longer!' By now, the rain had become a torrent, and everyone was soaked to the skin. But they still kept pulling. With the slight slope to navigate, it was some time before the bus finally reached the plot of land at the bottom of the embankment. Everyone was smeared with rain and mud. A few final adjustments were made until, finally, the bus was in position.

Before long, the rain dwindled, and clear patches began opening in the sky.

'That bus became our nursery school. I was the first headteacher.'

Shafts of light were piercing through the clouds.

'Now, seventy years later, there's a three-storey steel-reinforced concrete building here instead. But it all started with that bus.'

Meanwhile, the young Hatsue was standing proudly in front of the bus in question.

'That should do it! Thank you all very much for your help!'

There were cheers from all around the bus. The children started splashing around merrily in the newly formed puddles. Normally, that would have earned them a scolding, but everyone was already drenched anyway.

'Just look at us – we're soaked to the skin! You can't even tell if it's sweat or mud on my face!' said Hatsue, readying the camera. 'I have to say, though. We do look happy.'

She positioned the bus and crowd within the viewfinder. Pausing to wipe the corners of her eyes with a sleeve, she asked, 'This is the shutter, isn't it?'

'Yes, that one there,' said Hirasaka, pointing to the

button in question. Hatsue felt for it, then pressed it halfway down. She heard the lens whirring as it found focus. Then she pressed it all the way, and the shutter of the Canon Autoboy quietly clicked.

———

When the rain lifted, they began walking along the embankment again. A frog hopped out from among the glistening blades of grass. Was it her imagination, or had it noticed her presence? It hopped past her leg and then disappeared back into the long grass. A gentle breeze swept across the embankment.

Hirasaka looked at her as if to say: *Shall we get going?*

'Mr Hirasaka, if you don't mind . . . Seeing as we're here and everything, could we keep walking along the river until the sun goes down?'

The pleasant breeze, even the weeds growing along the bank – now that it came to it, she was reluctant to part with any of it. In the distance loomed the four Ghost Chimneys.

'When we started using the bus as the nursery, it was mayhem – especially on rainy days,' said Hatsue, squinting against the wind. 'The seats were our desks, the hanging straps our toys. It was small and cramped, but we were just happy to have a roof over our heads. Finally, we had our own nursery. After that, we held a night market or a jumble sale every year. There was even a sewing club where we collected and fixed old clothes. We kept saving and saving, and before too long we managed to build a wooden structure for the nursery.'

'A proper building, after all that time. You must have been delighted!'

'It even had a nice big hall, so the kids had somewhere to play indoors. After that, the next thing on our wish list was a piano. I'd always dreamed of buying one, and it would have been perfect for the hall.'

'A piano?'

'They were awfully expensive back then. We all assumed we'd never be able to afford one.'

'I can imagine.'

'We kept saving up for one. Then, when we did a fundraising drive, I spotted a certain someone on the list of donors. Mr Hirasaka, can you guess who it was?'

Seeing his puzzled look, she went ahead and told him.

'It was Mrs Hisano.'

'You mean . . . the lady who kept writing those angry notes? The one who kicked you off her land?'

'That's the one. I think she wanted somehow to make up for how she'd acted. In the end, she pulled some strings and managed to get one of the best pianos delivered to the nursery at a very good price. I only heard the full story much later. I imagine there was a bit of her usual

71

sarcasm mixed in there – you know, like she was hoping that this way we might at least sing in tune.'

Hatsue and Hirasaka looked out over the river. A boat was making its way downstream. Waves fanned out in its wake, glinting in the evening sun. The pair carried on gazing at the scene until, eventually, the waves disappeared.

———

Hatsue's perception seemed to sway and flicker, and then she was back in the white room at the photography studio. The door behind them had already shut.

'Well, Hatsue, please go ahead and choose your remaining photos. I'll get started on developing this film in the meantime.'

It seemed there was another small room alongside the equipment room. When Hirasaka opened the door, Hatsue glimpsed a strange red light and a row of unfamiliar equipment.

'This is the darkroom. I'll show you how everything works in a moment.'

'You actually use a darkroom? I don't know much about photos, but I thought it was all done by machines these days. So you're going to develop the film by hand?'

'That's right. Yes, you can get automatic processors and printers to do the job for you. But I . . .' Hirasaka trailed off mysteriously, as if unsure what to say next.

'You do it for the fun of it?' asked Hatsue.

'That's right. I suppose I just prefer it this way.'

Hatsue carried on sifting through the pile of photographs on the desk. Each triggered a flurry of memories. Slowly but surely, she picked out the ones that moved her the most.

A photo from when the wooden nursery building was completed. The new garden with its spindly freshly planted trees. The decorations for the graduation ceremony, and that shiny new piano. Even if she couldn't choose them all, they were the precious memories that made her who she was.

After a while, Hirasaka called out to her.

'Hatsue, the film is ready to start drying. Would you like to see the photo you took just now?'

She walked into the darkroom, where she was greeted by a peculiar smell, presumably that of the chemicals he was using.

Hirasaka was taking a pair of scissors to the film, which dangled in a long strip from the ceiling. As they were negatives and the colours were reversed, it was hard to tell whether her photos were any good.

In the sink was a square tray with two compartments, each filled with a strange-looking liquid – one red, and the other a dark purple. Next to them was another tray filled with water. A thin trickle of water was running from the tap.

'In order to help you choose your best shot, I'm going

to make you a contact sheet so you can see all your photos at once. I'll show you the process if you're interested. We're using colour film, so it'll have to be completely dark in here. Just give me a moment . . .'

She went and stood by his side, and then the lights went out, pitching the room into total darkness.

After a moment, there was a flash of light from one of the machines.

'Sorry about the dark. This'll just take a moment. First we soak the photographic paper in this colour developer, followed by a bleach-fix solution. Then we rinse it with water.'

She sensed Hirasaka moving about in the darkness. He seemed to be soaking the paper in the strange-coloured liquids.

'Here we go.'

Hatsue blinked as the lights came on. She looked down and saw a sheet of paper floating in the water. On it, framed in neat rows, were all the photographs she'd taken.

'My photos!' she exclaimed.

'I'll just dry them, and then you can choose which one you prefer.'

After removing the paper from the drying machine, Hirasaka handed her a special magnifying glass with which to inspect the rows of tiny photos. After some hesitation, she pointed at one of them.

'Ah,' nodded Hirasaka. 'I thought you might choose that one.'

It was the photo of everyone smiling in front of the newly installed bus.

'Right then. Let's try blowing it up to full size.'

She stood by Hirasaka's side as he set about producing larger versions of the photo, giving him detailed comments about which colours should be a little darker or lighter, or how a particular red could be a bit more intense.

'Thank you. It really does help knowing exactly how you'd like it.'

Before long, a small pile of rejects had formed.

'Isn't it a waste of paper, throwing all these away?'

'I wouldn't say so,' said Hirasaka, shaking his head. 'It's all part of the process if we want to get the best possible photo. If we compromise at this stage, we'll never get a decent result.'

By the time they'd finished tweaking the photograph and arrived at a version they were both happy with, a peculiar camaraderie had developed between them.

She peered at the finished photo.

The evening sun was slanting through the gaps that had opened in the clouds, streaking the scene with an almost celestial light. In the middle of the photograph was the bus, still glistening from the rain, the droplets on its windows testament to the intensity of the earlier downpour.

Hatsue was standing in front of the bus having just risen from a bow, an exhausted but joyful smile on her face. Her hair was plastered flat against her head, her clothes were sopping wet, and she looked generally rather scruffy. But, she thought, that might have been the biggest smile of my life. Around her stood the members of the parent–teacher association. There were the mothers in their smocks with the sleeves rolled up, and little Mii-chan's father, showing off his strong, thick arms. Mrs Sakaida was there in the corner, dressed in her usual fancy clothing despite the circumstances. The adults looked overcome with emotion, while the children were running around and splashing in the puddles.

'Thank you. I'm glad my last photo turned out so nicely.'

Hirasaka gave a satisfied nod. 'I'm happy to have been of service.'

Afterwards, Hatsue spent a very long time selecting her remaining ninety-one photographs. How long, she wasn't exactly sure. Here in the studio, her sense of time seemed to have faded. There was no day or night, nothing to remind her of the hours passing, nor did she ever feel sleepy. Stopping occasionally for a tea break or a chat, she slowly made her selection.

Now she was looking at her last photo. It showed her lying on a hospital bed during a visit by her sister and nephews. Hatsue hadn't been very tall to start with, but here she looked particularly small and shrivelled, like a balloon with no air left in it. Her sister was holding her hand, while her nephews dabbed at their eyes with handkerchiefs.

She counted the photos. Ninety, ninety-one, ninety-two. Yes, that was all of them.

'It must feel quite satisfying to have chosen all those,' said Hirasaka, gazing at the stack of photos by her side. He picked them up and went to sit at his workbench, where he began inspecting them one by one with his magnifying glass.

'I have to say I envy you,' murmured Hirasaka as he worked his way through the photos. He seemed to have relaxed slightly now that Hatsue had finished her selection. 'You asked me about my life earlier, didn't you?'

'Oh, don't worry,' she replied. 'I understand if you'd rather not talk about it.'

'Actually, the thing is . . . I don't remember it,' said Hirasaka, as he carefully poured some sort of chemical into a beaker.

'You don't . . . remember?'

'You see, after they die, people are always supposed to arrive here the way you did – armed with memories of their life, and the photos to match. Even those with dementia seem to regain their memory once they get here. Whoever you are, at the end of your life, you get to look back on

77

your life through photos – that's the rule. But in my case, there was nothing. No memories, no photos. I suppose there must have been some kind of mistake; in any case, my situation appears to be basically unprecedented. I turned up here with almost nothing. All I had in my hands was a single photo. Not a memory photo or anything – just a regular old photo. I'm in it, but I haven't the foggiest idea when it was taken, or by who.'

Oh my, thought Hatsue. 'What was in the photo? Maybe there are some clues in the background. And your clothes – wouldn't they at least let you guess roughly when it was taken?'

If Mr Hirasaka were a woman, she thought, it would probably be easier to tell from his hair or clothes what era he belonged to. Still, there had to be some kind of hint.

'I had the same idea, but it's no use. I can't remember a thing. The photo appears to have been taken in a forest somewhere, but . . .'

Hirasaka disappeared off somewhere to find the photo in question, before returning. The photo was framed in a white stand. And there he was, smiling out from the photo. It was black and white, and Hatsue couldn't tell if the background really was a forest as he claimed. But his hairstyle and clothing were exactly the same as they were now. Around his neck was the familiar stand-up collar of his white shirt.

It was hard to tell anything at all from the photo. The top of Hirasaka's head was visible, as if he was sitting down and the person who'd taken it was standing up. Other than that, it didn't seem to offer a single clue.

Hatsue handed the photo back to him.

'Mr Hirasaka, I'm sure you lived a good life before arriving here. You can tell from the photo – just look at that grin of yours!'

'You think so?' replied Hirasaka, glancing in her direction as he carried on tinkering with the machinery. 'Well, one thing is clear: I definitely wasn't some genius inventor, or a hero who died saving someone's life, or a famous manga artist whose death was mourned by the whole country . . .' Hirasaka's mouth had curled into a self-deprecatory grin.

'Oh, you never know – maybe you really were famous, and I just happen to have never heard of you.'

'I don't think so,' said Hirasaka, shaking his head. 'Hundreds and thousands of people have passed through here, more than I can count. If I was really that famous, I'm sure one of them would have thought to mention it! If I'd been successful in my work, or sociable enough to have plenty of friends, I'm sure someone would have recognized me by now. And if there was anything I was really passionate about, then surely something would have reminded me of it. No, I probably just led an ordinary life and then shuffled off the mortal coil without anyone even noticing. A boring old existence, with nothing to show for it. In fact, maybe I'm better off not knowing.'

For a moment, Hatsue didn't know what to say.

'But,' she began, surprised by the loudness of her own voice. 'Look at it this way: at least that means you weren't some mass-murdering villain, or a convict on death row! In a way, isn't that nice to know?'

Hirasaka chuckled. 'I suppose you're right.' The machine still whirring, he carried on working as he spoke, his hands moving dexterously about. 'I just tell myself that as long as I keep seeing people off like this, I'm bound to suddenly remember something, or bump into someone who knows me.'

'Well, if you'd been one of the kids at my nursery, I'd have remembered every little thing about you. Whether you liked playing on stilts, or were a fast runner – that kind of thing.'

'Thank you for saying that. I don't really have any ties to the world of the living, so I wouldn't mind moving on to the afterlife, even without my memory. But it all just seems a little . . . sad. I find myself wondering what it even means for me to die if I don't remember anything and nobody knows who I was. A boring life, a boring death, and no one to ever remember me. Is there any meaning or purpose to my existence that way? Why was I even alive in the first place?'

Hatsue mulled his words. *A meaning or purpose to his existence* . . . There are certain points in life, she thought, when you have the chance to give someone the small gift of a few carefully considered words. She didn't know if she'd be able to find them, but she knew that now was one of those times.

'You know, I saw countless children through nursery. Later, some of them were very successful in life, others less so. But to me, every single one of their lives was like a precious little jewel. They didn't have to make it big. They didn't have to become famous. And you see, getting to speak with you, Mr Hirasaka, at the end of my life – it really has made me very happy.'

Still facing away from her, Hirasaka went quiet, as though deep in thought.

'Thank you. Hearing you say that makes me very happy, too.' He nodded gently, then fell silent again.

The spinning lantern was complete. Studded with various colours, it resembled an enormous, intricately cut gemstone.

'How beautiful.'

The lantern was covered with the photos of her most cherished memories. Each of them seemed to emit its own beautiful glow.

'I'd like you to concentrate on the lantern until it stops spinning. When that happens, you'll be on your way.'

Hirasaka walked over to the lantern and placed a hand on its frame.

'Well, off we go!'

A mechanism of some kind hummed into life. As the lantern spun, its light shone through the photos, scattering beams of coloured light across the room.

Birth. Her mother and father, cradling Hatsue's tiny body like it was the most precious thing in the world.

One year old. Sitting on the veranda, her little belly bathed in sunlight.

Two years old. Asleep on her mother's back, her neck cocked to one side.

The lantern kept spinning. She was shown times when, miraculously, everything went according to plan, and times when nothing did. Moments that were painful to remember, and wonderful experiences that it soothed her to recall.

Twenty-six years old. Looking shy at her wedding. That all-white kimono never did suit her.

She watched as the photographs whirled past, each a tiny snippet of her life infused with its own particular radiance.

Thirty-four years old. The nursery they'd finally managed to build, looking like it was about to be swept away in a flood. With water up to their knees, everyone was helping to heave the precious piano up onto a platform.

'Children really are worth whatever it takes. If I'm reincarnated, I hope I get to be a nursery teacher again.'

'I'll have my fingers crossed!' said Hirasaka, who was standing in the corner of the room to watch. His face, too, was bathed in the colours of the lantern.

'You look after yourself, you hear? Don't work too hard,' Hatsue called over to him.

'Yes, Miss Mishima!' he replied. As he turned to face her, his face crumpled into a smile that was different, somehow, from the more neutral expression he'd shown her so far. She was glad she'd had the chance to see it before she went.

'There's plenty I still wanted to do, but I'm happy with my lot. I really am glad I got to meet you at the end like this, Mr Hirasaka.'

'Oh, me too.'

Still gazing at the lantern, Hatsue fell silent for a moment. Then she added: 'I hope you find what you're looking for.'

As the lantern slowed, the photos became more and more vivid, seeming to fill her field of vision.

'Ah. The last photo.'

It was the photo of everyone smiling in front of the bus.

The light grew brighter and brighter, until Hatsue felt it enveloping her entire consciousness.

Then, without a sound, the lantern came to a halt.

———— • ————

As the light intensified, the room became bathed in whiteness. Hatsue's figure faded into the light, and by the time it had subsided, she was nowhere to be seen.

Hirasaka was alone in the room again. He had lit a small lamp and was filling out a form.

Hatsue's lantern had stopped spinning, but it was still casting an array of colours onto the white floor. The sight of it plunged him into contemplation.

How very like Hatsue to spend her last moments worrying about someone other than herself, he thought. The children she'd taught must have been lucky to have her.

She seemed to have departed for the afterlife without any regrets. Plenty of his other visitors refused, at first, to accept the fact that they'd died. When they realized they were stuck here with no way back, they would quietly give up on everything. And that process of giving up was, ultimately, how they became ready to move on. Hirasaka's job was to patiently accompany the dead through that process of anger and grief.

Sometimes he spoke gently with them, listening for

hours as they talked about every single one of their grudges and gripes, or tearfully ran through the list of all the things they'd still wanted to do. Sometimes he just stayed at their side as they cried and cried for their family. Sometimes he even rubbed their backs until they felt better.

At first, he had simply pasted the automatically printed photos onto a rudimentary lantern, without making any adjustments. Eventually, however, this endless assembly line of memories began to wear him down. It was like a closed loop with no way out, and some part of him was quietly going haywire. It was then that Hirasaka discovered the pleasures of working in the darkroom, which became his one source of enjoyment.

In that gloomy space, he would dip the photographic paper into the developing solution and wait for an image to appear on the surface of the photographic paper. He would make adjustments, drawing out a certain figure, toning the background down, emphasizing a particular patch of light. Considering each photograph a work of art, he would ask himself how he could make it as beautiful as it could be. He did this for the dead – these were the last images they would see before the afterlife, after all – but he also did it for himself.

He did it so that he could continue down this road, which was so long it had begun to feel endless. So that he could keep himself in one piece.

One by one, the dead passed through his studio, each of their photos filling it with a brief glimmer of life.

Would his own memories ever return, he wondered?

When he had finished filling out his paperwork, Hirasaka got to his feet. Thinking he'd have a cup of coffee in the waiting room, he went to fetch his bean grinder.

His eyes landed on the photo again. There he was, in black and white, smiling at the camera. He must have looked at this photo thousands, if not tens of thousands of times. Hirasaka closed his eyes.

Who was that smile for? And where did this photo even come from?

He simply didn't know.

All Hirasaka could do was wait, endlessly, for that *someone* to arrive. The person who could tell him who he was.

By the time he opened his eyes, he'd probably have a new visitor on his hands. So, for just a moment longer, he decided to keep them shut.

———•———

Hatsue felt herself falling.

When she opened her eyes, she found herself standing in front of her nursery school. It seemed that rather than haunting someone at their bedside, as was considered usual, it was the school that had her attention, right to the end.

86

A young woman was standing in front of the school, wearing a suit and a slightly oversized pair of pumps. She kept glancing down at her watch, a tense expression lining her features. Hatsue guessed that she was interviewing for a job at the school. She was probably about to meet the headteacher.

Looking down at a notepad, she seemed to be learning her lines.

My name is Michi . . . Thank you for the opportunity . . . The reason I applied is . . . My strengths include my perseverance . . .

Curious what else might be written on the notepad, Hatsue made her way over, but the woman started on the spot and looked right at her.

'Um, g-good morning!'

So the woman could see her, then.

'Good morning,' she replied. 'Are you applying to be a teacher?'

The woman seemed even more surprised. 'H-how did you know? That's right. I'm interviewing today.' Her teeth were practically chattering from nerves.

'I might be an old lady now, but I taught here back in the day.'

A smile rose to the woman's face. 'Oh! Was it . . . hard work?'

'Oh, it's a tough job. Bad for your back too. But

children are such fun. Every day is different. After all, they're worth whatever it takes.'

The woman nodded and looked over at the nursery. She had nice eyes, thought Hatsue – nervous, but brimming with hope.

'I've heard this school has quite a history.'

Hatsue nodded. *Oh yes. More than you could know*. She wanted to tell the woman all sorts of things. But instead she simply smiled and said: 'Well, good luck, Miss Michi.'

'Thank you very – wait, where did . . .'

Hatsue was no longer visible, it seemed. The woman was glancing around, as though baffled by her abrupt disappearance. Then she looked at her watch, gasped, and hurried off towards the school.

The voices of children echoed high into the blue sky. I've got a long journey ahead of me, thought Hatsue to herself, I might as well have one last look. And she followed the woman inside.

Chapter Two

The Hero and the Mouse

Seen through the windows of the photo studio, the outside world always seemed to be on the cusp of nightfall. The gloaming, as one of Hirasaka's guests had told him it was called. The in-between time that joined day and night. It was during the gloaming, apparently, that all sorts of spirits came out to play.

A shape darted past the window outside. Barely an instant later, there was a cheerful flurry of knocks at the door.

'Delivery for you, Mr Hirasaka!' came the usual voice.

Impressed, as always, by the delivery man's unfailing cheerfulness, Hirasaka opened the door.

Waiting outside was Yama, wearing his usual uniform

with the cap turned backwards, his faithful trolley at his side.

'Your next guest is a strapping young man, by the look of things.'

'Won't fool me that easily,' smiled Hirasaka as he signed for the delivery. 'From the size of this package, he must be well into middle age.'

'You got me. Plus, guess what? This is a red-sticker case. Looks like you're in for a rough ride.'

Sure enough, there was a red sticker on top of the file that Yama handed him. This was a warning that the guest in question hadn't died by accident or from natural causes, but through murder or suicide – in other words, at human hands.

Yama was visibly excited about this development – presumably because it was Hirasaka's problem to deal with, not his.

'How did he die? Some kind of . . . altercation?' asked Hirasaka.

'Bzz – wrong answer!'

'Come on,' sighed Hirasaka. 'This isn't a quiz show.'

His usual policy was to avoid forming any preconceptions by looking at his guests' files in advance, preferring instead to get to know them through friendly conversation. That way, he avoided any judgements on what type of person they were. More often than not, those sorts of hasty, superficial assumptions tended to be proven wrong eventually, and got in the way of a smooth send-off.

But with red-sticker guests, it was worth finding out at least a little in advance.

Yama scanned through the file, then continued his performance.

'The correct answer is . . . a stabbing! A sword in the back, to be precise. Guy died from fatal blood loss.'

Just hearing this made Hirasaka want to bury his head in his hands. Yes, this was going to be a tough one. Of course, the man wouldn't arrive still covered in blood or anything – his guests always arrived looking just as they had in their prime. Still, for someone who'd died that way, looking back on life wasn't likely to be a very tranquil or enjoyable affair. Stabbed in the back with a sword . . . it sounded like something from another era.

'Did you say a sword? Is he from the modern day?'

'Oh, yes.'

'Is he . . . yakuza, then?'

'Well, he sure looks the part . . .' said Yama, closing the file and tucking it under his arm.

Hirasaka picked up the box of the photos and tested its weight. 'By the way, Mr Yama, how long are *you* planning on sticking around here? You've been doing this for quite a while, haven't you?'

Yama had been here since before Hirasaka took over at

the studio. He looked and acted young enough, but Hirasaka had never really thought about how long he might have actually been here. When he himself had first arrived, it had been Yama who had shown him the ropes, the rules, what was expected of him – and how to guide people into the afterlife.

'What can I say?' replied Yama. 'I like the job. Delivering photos all over the place – it suits me, somehow.'

Hirasaka himself was unable to step outside, so he'd never seen them, but apparently there were plenty of other photography studios just like his. Presumably, their purpose was the same as his: to send people off into the afterlife.

'Right then,' said Yama, adjusting his cap. 'I should get on with my next delivery. No rest for the wicked, eh? Even if time's stopped, they somehow manage to keep us busy . . .'

With a brief wave, Yama disappeared into the gloom.

Hirasaka prepared the room for his next guest. Shohei Waniguchi, stabbed to death with a sword. Hirasaka hoped he'd be able to give him a decent send-off, with just the right photos.

And maybe this time, he thought, something will trigger my memories, and I'll finally remember who I am.

———•———

Waniguchi opened his eyes.

As he sat up, he noticed a strange man smiling politely at him.

'Welcome,' said the man. 'I'm glad you made it.'

Waniguchi sprang to his feet in an instant. He glanced right, ducked left, and slid a hand around the man's back. From there it was easy enough to get an arm around his neck and put him in a chokehold.

A walkover, in other words.

'Alright, mister,' he murmured in the man's ear, slowly tightening his hold. 'What's your game?'

Waniguchi was good at making snap decisions. He'd woken up in a room he didn't recognize, which could only mean one thing: he'd been drugged and abducted. And *that* meant that whatever happened next wasn't going to be much fun. Torture, for example. Maybe even a straight-up execution. Waniguchi worked all this out within a matter of seconds. The key, in situations like this, was to fight back quickly.

The man was gasping by this point, so Waniguchi relaxed his hold slightly.

'Please,' said the man. 'Violence won't get you—'

'Oi! I'll shut you up for good if you're not careful!'

'Actually . . . the thing is . . . we're both already dead . . .'

Waniguchi slackened his hold on the man, who slumped to the ground in a squat. He had bony shoulders.

'What do you mean, I'm dead?' asked Waniguchi, looking down at the man. He had positioned his boot close to the man's fingers, ready to stamp on them at a moment's notice.

'Yes, Mr Waniguchi. You're dead. You died just a moment ago, in fact. Is that ringing any bells?'

Come to think of it, it was.

Someone had stabbed him from behind. For a moment, all he'd felt was hot. Not painful – just hot. He'd seen something sharp and bloody protruding from his stomach before realizing it was the tip of a sword. After that, all he'd felt was a cold sensation spreading through his body.

'That . . . that really happened? And now I'm dead?'

'That's right,' said the man as he slowly rose from where he'd been crouched, rubbing his neck. 'It happened just now. That's why you're here.'

Waniguchi rubbed his belly, but could feel no wound or pain.

'So who are you? God or something?'

As he stared at the man, he wondered what would happen if, at this point, he decided to kill 'God'. The man must have sensed this, because he began backing away from him.

'No, no – I'm a regular human just like you. Nothing more than a sort of guide, really. But if you keep trying to hurt me like that, it won't end very well for you. You'll be stuck here for ever.'

'You trying to threaten me?'

He grabbed the man by the scruff of the neck and gave him a good stare, but he didn't even flinch. Waniguchi's stare was usually capable of putting the fear into most people, but the man seemed immune to its effects. Well, if they were both already half dead – fully dead, in fact – then torturing him probably wouldn't achieve anything. Even his favourite expression – *You're a dead man!* – wouldn't have the same ring to it here.

He released the man's collar.

'My name is Hirasaka,' said the man, smoothing out his clothes. 'My job is to give everyone who passes through this photo studio a pleasant send-off.'

'Huh? A send-off? To *where*?'

'The . . . other world, so to speak.'

'What's the point? I already know I'm going straight to hell.'

Waniguchi's criminal record ranged from minor misdemeanours to serious offences, and was so long he couldn't even remember the whole list. In his line of work, violence was generally considered a good thing, which explained how he'd racked up so many grudges in his time. Back in the world of the living, plenty of people were probably raising a glass to his early departure.

'I myself don't know much about your final destination – other than what I've gleaned from hearsay. But from what I *have* heard, there's no neat division between heaven and hell.'

'How's it work then?'

'Why don't you relax a little first?' said Hirasaka, gesturing towards the interior of the studio. 'Can I make you a coffee?'

'What, you don't have any booze in this place?'

'Oh, I do. All sorts, in fact.'

'How about some Booker's?' Waniguchi asked, trying the name of his favourite bourbon.

'Certainly. Please, come on in.'

Waniguchi followed Hirasaka into the studio.

Despite his recent demise, the Booker's tasted as good as usual as it slid down his throat. The same warming sensation, the same pleasant fire in his stomach. The bourbon drifted down through the ice cubes like a fine mist.

'Got any snacks to go with this?'

Hirasaka brought him some beef jerky. He tore off a piece with his teeth and felt its intense, meaty flavour fill his mouth.

'Sorry if I was a little rough on you just now,' said Waniguchi. 'Come on, drink with me.'

'Alright then.'

Hirasaka's features remained composed as he sipped on the bourbon. It seemed the man could hold his drink.

'So. I'm dead, eh?'

Even saying it out loud, it didn't feel very real. The richly flavoured jerky, the fiery bourbon . . . they tasted exactly like they always had.

'Yes, unfortunately. This studio is a sort of staging post between life and death.'

Waniguchi had never stepped foot anywhere near a photography studio before. His main experience of photographs had been in the form of glaring mug shots.

'Why a photography studio? What am I supposed to do here, eh?'

Hirasaka refilled his drink. 'Actually, Mr Waniguchi, I'd like you to choose some photos for me. One for every year you were alive – so forty-seven in total.'

'Me, choose photos? Nah. You go ahead and pick 'em if you like.'

'The thing is, it sort of has to be you. It's your lantern we're making, after all.'

'The hell are you on about? Anyway, what if it's a baby or something that winds up here? *They* ain't going to pick their own photos, are they?'

The question seemed to startle Hirasaka. But it seemed like a pretty obvious one to Waniguchi – if, as the man claimed, all sorts of people arrived here.

'Well, in that case, I usually hold them and get them to pick a photo.'

'Do they even know what they're doing?'

'Oh yes. They try and grab the photos. Sometimes they smile at them.'

Huh, thought Waniguchi quite solemnly. Something was wrong with the world if there were babies dying young while *he*, of all people, got to live to the ripe old age of forty-seven.

Next, Hirasaka began explaining how they would build his memory lantern. By the time he had finished, Waniguchi was emptying the packet of beef jerky into his mouth.

'And I choose the photos. Forty-seven of 'em.'

'That's right.'

'And at the end I have to watch the lantern spin and think about my life.'

'Exactly.'

'Jeez. Sounds like a drag. Count me out.'

Hirasaka visibly struggled to stifle a sigh. 'Please, Mr Waniguchi, don't be like that.'

Waniguchi sank into thought. *My whole life was probably a mistake, right from the point of conception. Or maybe my mum just raised me wrong. Either way, I ended up with exactly the shoddy life I deserved, so all this crap about looking back on it sounds pretty damn meaningless.* He found himself rubbing the sword wound on his cheek. It was an old wound, but the skin there was still visibly indented, and felt different to the touch.

'If you don't, you'll never be able to leave this studio. Please, at least give it a little thought.'

'There any women in this place?'

'None.'

Waniguchi found himself glaring at Hirasaka. I wish *he* was a woman, he thought. That would have made this a bit more fun, at least.

Hirasaka clasped his hands together awkwardly. 'Well . . .'

'So . . . I can't move on until I've chosen the photos.'

'Exactly,' said Hirasaka, a note of relief in his voice.

'Well then, looks like I got no choice. Bring 'em over and let's get this over with, okay?'

And so Waniguchi began sorting through the photos of his life.

Spread out on the desk, their sheer number surprised him. One for every day of his life – including plenty from the distant past. Seeing himself as a kid again, standing in that shabby ground-floor apartment, was a pretty strange experience. Back then, he didn't have the scar on his cheek. Or the tattoos all over his shoulders and back. And, of course, he still had his little finger. A normal enough kid, basically – apart from that fiery look in his eyes, maybe.

'I have to choose from these photos?'

Hirasaka nodded. 'Yes. And then, before you leave here,

you'll watch them spin around on the lantern, and look back on your life.'

'I couldn't care less about my life.' After all, it wasn't like he'd done anything special.

'Be that as it may, these photos are a record of your existence,' said Hirasaka. 'I'll help build the lantern itself. Now, please take a look in here.'

He opened the door to a perfectly square room, every inch of which was pure white. It's like one of those psych wards for junkies, thought Waniguchi.

'You'll view the lantern in there.'

'Whatever,' muttered Waniguchi with a nod, before returning to the photos and spreading them out on the desk with both hands.

'Woah,' he said, raising his voice. 'What the . . .'

The photo he was looking at showed him being carried out of a room, his stomach a bloody mess.

'Ah, yes, sorry about that. You see, the photos cover your entire life, which includes the day you died.'

'I mean, I know it's me and everything, but that's pretty . . . gross.'

He could also make out a pair of black shoes in the corner of the photo. They looked familiar.

Of course, he'd been there too. The Mouse.

'Ah, there we go,' he said, soon finding the photo he was looking for. The goggling eyes, the small, buck-toothed mouth. That hunch, discernible even in a photo. The wide forehead, the tiny, jutting chin. The thin, barely visible layer of hair on his head. The enormous, floppy ears. His whole appearance was just so . . . mouse-like.

'Your brother?' asked Hirasaka.

'You kidding? Nah, that's the Mouse.'

'The Mouse?'

'His real name's Michiya, but just look at him: 100 per cent mouse, right? The guy worked for me. We never called him Michiya or anything – it was always "the Mouse". He was a repairman. Total oddball. Like talking to an alien. Sure knew how to fix things, though.' Waniguchi sank into thought. By this point, he was talking to himself more than Hirasaka.

'I wonder if there's a photo of the day we . . .' he said, rummaging through the photos again. 'Ah, here we go . . . wait, why's it all faded, huh?' His tone had suddenly become threatening again.

The middle of the photo in question was a white blur, as if a bright light had been shining at the camera. Three pairs of feet were all that was visible. Still, it was possible to distinguish one pair of snakeskin boots, one pair of black canvas shoes, and one pair of what were clearly children's shoes.

'Well,' Hirasaka explained hastily, 'you know how the photos you treasure the most are the ones you always get out to look at, so they end up all faded and torn? Well, it's the same with memories.'

'Huh. Fat lot of use, then,' said Waniguchi, clicking his tongue in irritation.

'But don't worry. There's a way we can restore this photo.'

'Restore this piece of crap? How?'

'We can go back in time – just for one day, mind – and retake the photo in question. The same place, the same time – with whatever camera you'd like.'

Going back into the past? Back to the day that photo was taken?

'Well, what do you say?'

'Hmm . . .' murmured Waniguchi, glancing back down at the photo of the Mouse. 'The thing is, I'm not *that* desperate to go back and see the guy . . .'

'Right then. We'll stay here.'

'Wait,' said Waniguchi. 'I . . . guess we might as well. Ain't like there's anything to do here anyway. Might as well make my peace with the world of the living.' He pointed at the photograph. 'We took this on Christmas Eve, see. Me, the Mouse, and that kid – a customer of ours, actually. We were in the office at the time.'

'I see,' said Hirasaka, scribbling something in a notepad. 'Well, we have just about every camera you can think of, so please let me know if there's a particular type you'd like to use. This way, please,' said Hirasaka, getting up and beckoning him towards another room. 'This is the equipment room. If you like, I can pick one out for you based on your preferences. You know, something that'll be easy for you to use . . .'

'My preferences? What, you want me to actually take the photo? Nah, you take it for me.'

'Now, now. There are rules, I'm afraid. If you're recreating a photo, you have to be the one to take it.'

As he spoke, Hirasaka opened the door to the equipment room. Sure enough, the shelves inside were lined with an enormous variety of cameras.

'Well, if you insist . . .' said Waniguchi, crossing his arms as he pondered the options. 'Right then. Leica IIf with an Elmar lens. Make it an f2.8.'

Hirasaka seemed stunned. 'Mr Waniguchi . . . you're a camera fan? How wonderful!'

'Not exactly. The Mouse, right, he repaired a camera like that once. Started murmuring about how beautiful it was. So I couldn't help remembering it. We sold plenty of cameras like that at the shop too. "Leica IIf with an Elmar f2.8." He just sounded so funny saying it.'

'Well, it's an exquisite combination. I'll just fetch that for you, then.'

When Hirasaka reappeared and handed him the Leica, he found that it fit snugly in his hand. Its rounded body had a satisfying weight, the kind that made you never want to put it down. He tried the winding lever and shutter release, and was pleasantly surprised by how smooth and un-mechanical it all felt. He pressed the shutter a few more times.

'Yeah, this'll do.'

Hirasaka seemed relieved by his initial reaction.

Waniguchi peered through the viewfinder of the Leica. He tried focusing on Hirasaka, eventually resolving the two identical faces in the viewfinder into a single one that looked back at him.

'Hey, mister,' he said, holding out the camera, 'stick some film in here, would you?'

'Certainly.' Hirasaka took the camera over to a counter in the room. Peering over, Waniguchi saw him carefully trimming the edges of a roll of film. He remembered the Mouse doing something similar whenever he tested one of the cameras he was repairing.

'And I don't know much about exposure or anything. When it's crunch time, you'll sort the settings and focus out for me, won't you?'

'Of course,' nodded Hirasaka as he gently loaded the film into the Leica. 'This way, please,' he called, ushering Waniguchi towards the door in the white room. They stood in front of it, shoulder to shoulder.

'Right then. The twenty-fourth of December last year – from the first ray of morning sunshine to dawn the next day. Does that sound right to you?'

'Sure,' nodded Waniguchi.

'Well then, we're off to spend a day with Mr Mouse, repairman extraordinaire.'

'It's just "the Mouse", actually.'

'My apologies. A day with the Mouse, then.'

Hirasaka opened the door.

———

We going for a walk or something? thought Waniguchi.

But as soon as he stepped through the door, he found himself in Kita-Senju, right in the middle of the morning rush hour. When he turned around, the door they'd just walked through was nowhere to be seen. The sun had barely risen, but there were a huge number of commuters bustling about. Good for them, he thought. Bizarrely enough, people kept passing right through him. He even deliberately tried bumping someone's shoulder, to no avail. Normally, crowds like these would part fearfully as he strode along – but everyone was just passing right on by. In life, if someone with their eyes glued to their phone had bumped into him, it would be the start of an educational experience for them; alas, he was already dead.

'What's the deal, mister? That photo only happens later today. Do we just sit around until then?'

'My apologies. Returning to a precise time of day is rather difficult, which is why we always start at sunrise.

This is your last chance to say goodbye to the world of the living. Might I suggest you relax and try to enjoy the time you have?'

From the elevated walkway they were standing on they could see Kita-Senju station, all decked out for Christmas. Green, red, gold and silver; plastic Santas decorated with cotton snow. No one was looking at any of it, though – they were all too busy hurrying down the street to work. He sat there with Hirasaka and watched the crowds.

'Hey, how 'bout a drink? Ain't like there's much else to do.'

'Certainly. I'll just get us something.'

Hirasaka followed one of the commuters into a nearby convenience store. Waniguchi decided to tag along, mainly because he was curious about how they were going to manage to buy anything.

'I mean, everyone just passes right through us, and we can't talk to 'em either. How'd you expect this to work?'

'You know the offerings of food and drink that people leave in front of graves or family altars? Well, none of that goes to waste,' replied Hirasaka mysteriously.

He reached towards one of the beers in the display refrigerator. It was a special Christmas edition. 'Right now, we're formless beings – spirits, if you like. Which means that if I concentrate hard enough on the form of this can, and focus on extracting only the contents . . .' He carefully grasped the can. As he gently pulled on it, the can seemed to separate into two identical versions of itself – one still on the shelf, and one in his hand. 'There we go.'

Waniguchi tried it himself, but it was harder than it looked.

'Well, get me one of these, one of these . . . and these. Oh, this too,' he said, gesturing to a 'One Cup' jar of sake and various snacks. Hirasaka gathered the requested items in his arms, together with a few of his own choices.

'So we can just help ourselves to all this stuff without getting busted? Neat.'

'Well, we are dead, after all . . .'

Hirasaka and Waniguchi decided to hold their impromptu picnic on the middle of a pedestrian bridge. The centre-piece was a pack of sliced roast chicken.

'Merry Christmas!' said Waniguchi.

Hirasaka seemed a little startled, but eventually replied: 'Merry Christmas.' There was a pleasing hiss as they cracked open their cans.

For a while, they simply sipped their beers in silence, watching the crowds of commuters.

'Sweet potato fries and . . . sweet potato tart. You really like your sweet potato, huh?' said Waniguchi. Hirasaka's selection looked like the kind of thing a teenage girl might pick. 'Not exactly your usual beer snacks, are they . . .?'

'Sorry. I couldn't resist picking a few things for myself.'

'Hey, mister, tell me. You're dead, too, right? How'd you die – was it some kinda accident? I mean, you're pretty young . . .'

He'd only asked to pass the time. But Hirasaka's expression clouded over.

'Funnily enough, I don't actually remember.'

'What d'you mean, you don't remember?'

Hirasaka began to explain. How he didn't recall a thing about his life or death; how all he could do was keep fulfilling his role as guide in the vague hope that one day someone would come along who could tell him who he was. And how his only possession was a single photo.

'Hmm . . .' sighed Waniguchi. 'Well, I don't think you're famous. I ain't seen you on TV.' It was like Hirasaka said: he must have just been some nondescript, average sort of guy. 'Still, I know one thing, and that's that there are two types of people in life: those who deserve a beating, and those who don't. And guess what? You're firmly in the second category, my friend.'

'Really? You can tell a thing like that, can you?'

'Oh yeah. I've been round the block, you know. I can tell with a glance. Bad guys always have this look about them. Whereas you . . .' Hirasaka was staring intently at him. He lit a cigarette. 'I reckon you lived a decent life, and died a decent death. Ain't that enough?'

The smoke from his cigarette drifted up into the air.

For a while, they simply sat there on the bridge, quietly watching the throngs of people. Seeing how Hirasaka had clammed up, Waniguchi suddenly shoved the packet he was holding into his guide's pocket.

'How's that, eh? A little treat to take back with you.'

Hirasaka screwed up his face into an odd expression, somewhere between a grimace and a smile. It seemed he wanted to steer the conversation in a different direction.

'You know, I'm more interested in hearing about that repair whizz you mentioned. I mean, he's the one we're going to photograph later, isn't he?'

'Ah, the Mouse, eh? Yeah, real genius, that guy.'

And so, little by little, Waniguchi began to tell the strange story of the Mouse.

———•———

I could talk about the Mouse for hours and still not be done. The guy's that much of an oddball.

See, recently, it's been getting harder and harder to tap people for protection money. Other sources of income are hard to come by, too. So, for whatever reason, I was put in charge of a second-hand repair shop. Course, I didn't have to actually deal with customers or anything – I just ran things behind the scenes. The idea was that it would be an online-only operation, and basically serve as a front for us to move cash around. Cameras, watches, antiques – stuff like that has no fixed value, see, which makes it perfect for when you need to make large sums of money vanish. So the idea was that we'd trade in second-hand goods without actually running a physical shop. That's how Andromeda Used Goods was born.

The shop itself ran pretty smoothly. The thing was, we needed to do at least a little bit of business to avoid attracting attention. So, for the sake of appearances, we decided to hire someone who actually knew how to repair things.

Now, anyone with a few brain cells took one look at the run-down warehouse and its piles of junk awaiting repair – most of it stuff we'd taken in lieu of debt payments, or other objects of uncertain and likely illegal origin – and the general vibe given off by the young guy working under me (Kosaki, his name was) and worked out what was really going on. They'd say no thank you, the job's not for me, and head on home.

What's that? Nah, I didn't do the interviews myself. That was Kosaki. But I'd go up to him afterwards, give him a little slap on the head, and say: 'It's that look in your eyes that's putting them all off, you idiot!'

Then, one day, the Mouse turns up. The guy had gradu-ated from some kind of special school, and I wasn't so sure hiring someone like that was a good idea, but then he was only going to serve as a sort of fake repairman, and he wouldn't have to interact with any customers, so in the end we decided to hire him. He was almost thirty, but his old man – real feeble guy – still came with him to the interview. Kept bowing his head, saying his son was the best damn repairman in the world and would work real hard. Maybe he needed the cash or something. Still, Kosaki agreed the kid was worth a shot, and that was that.

Now, the whole time we were talking, the Mouse kept glancing around, sort of like he was scoping the place out. It was his dad who did all the talking – the kid stayed zipped the whole time.

Next day, the Mouse turns up with this backpack full of tools, and these two enormous toolboxes, one in each hand. I've never seen so many tools. He wasn't a big guy, so he sort of tottered about. He starts tidying up the repair counter, then he gets out a bunch of those triangular flasks people use for science experiments, and all sorts of other tools and screws and things. And he arranges them all with this incredible precision. I'm talking down to the *millimetre*.

'Oi, Mouse,' says Kosaki, who's technically his boss. 'Aren't you gonna say hello?'

See, Kosaki couldn't stand the fact that the guy wouldn't show him the proper respect. To a yakuza, hierarchy is everything. It doesn't matter if you're running some bogus repair shop – you still have to respect your superiors. But the Mouse, he just sort of ignored him, almost like he hadn't heard.

'You little . . .' says Kosaki. The guy had a short fuse – which is probably why he never made it very far up the ranks. So he grabs the Mouse by the collar, practically hoists him off the ground. But all the Mouse says is: 'Does something need fixing?'

'I ain't talking about fixing anything, dumbo,' says Kosaki. 'I'm talking about showing your boss a little respect.'

In our line of work, honour is important. If you ain't getting the respect you're due, you're basically toast.

Now, the Mouse was a strange kid. Most people would be shaking in their boots if a yakuza grabbed their collar and started threatening them. But he just stared right back at Kosaki with those dark little eyes of his.

'Oi, show some respect!' shouted Kosaki.

'Does something need fixing?' replied the Mouse. 'Or not?'

I decided to intervene. Otherwise, it looked like our precious repairman was going to take a beating, and things could get out of hand quick. So I came out from the office and shouted: 'Pack it in!'

Kosaki let go of the Mouse right away. The Mouse, meanwhile, still didn't seem to know the meaning of fear.

'Mouse, you have to greet people when you see them, okay?' I said in my loudest, most authoritative voice. Always best to go easy on the younger ones, I figured. 'Got that? You have to *greet* them,' I repeated emphatically.

But the Mouse just repeated: 'Does something need fixing?'

This was starting to rub even me the wrong way. Kosaki was looking at me with a face that said: *See what I mean?*

'Repeat after me, alright? Good morning.'

The Mouse seemed to think for a moment. Then he said: 'Is that necessary?'

The question took me by surprise a little, mainly because I'd begun to assume that the only words that ever came out of his mouth were *Does something need fixing?*

'Oh, it's necessary.'

'Why is it necessary?'

'Why . . . well . . .'

Why *was* it necessary? I didn't know what to tell him. I could have just given him a slap on the head and shouted at him to do as he was told. But even then, there was no telling what kind of response I'd get from the guy.

It was a feeling I hadn't really known since making it to the middle ranks of my organization. Probably a sort of fear, on some level. The Mouse made me feel like I'd come up against some entirely new type of human, a kind I'd never met before.

'It's necessary because . . . it makes me and Kosaki here feel good, okay?'

'And it's good to feel good?'

'Yeah. Think of it like fixing something. But invisible, and inside us.'

I'd said the first thing that came into my head, but I couldn't help feeling pleased with this line.

'Fixing something,' repeated the Mouse.

I decided to test him. 'Good morning!' I said.

'Good morning,' the Mouse replied, before turning politely to Kosaki. 'Good morning.' He paused. 'Did that fix you inside?'

'Sure, it fixed us inside. And your first job when you come in every morning is to fix me and Kosaki, alright?'

'Understood. You were broken. I fixed you.'

I couldn't help but grin. It was true, in a way – we were both probably pretty kaput on the inside.

The Mouse sat down and silently carried on arranging his tools. Kosaki and I exchanged a look.

'Just make sure you do a good job, okay?' I said in a low voice.

The workshop was in a converted factory on the outskirts of town, and faced onto a depressing little street that hardly anyone ever walked down. We'd taken the place over after seizing it from its previous owner. It was a two-storey building. The ground floor was the workshop – though it was more like a big warehouse really, filled with mysterious coils of wire, objects stolen from who knows where, and various stuff we'd seized as collateral. Upstairs was the office, which must have been added later, because it was a lot newer. Access between the two floors was via a sort of fire escape on the outside of the building. The office had a window built into the floor – I guess for keeping an eye on the workshop.

At first, Kosaki kept checking on Mouse from above, but eventually he got bored and went back to surfing the internet. Meanwhile, the Mouse was constantly busy tinkering with one thing or another.

'The kid sure knows how to concentrate,' Kosaki told me. 'He's been like that all day.'

As top dog, there was no need for me to spend all day hanging around in the office, but I was too intrigued by the Mouse's odd behaviour to go anywhere else.

'I'll go check on him,' I said, and headed down to the workshop.

Watching him from up close, I was blown away. I saw this thing on TV once about the robots that assemble electric appliances in factories. Always with the same speed and precision. No stopping to rest, no slowing down. It was just like that. The Mouse had found a relatively new DVD recorder – probably not even a type he'd come across before – and dismantled the whole thing in minutes. He never stopped to think, as if he knew the whole procedure like the back of his hand. Even laid out all the parts at equal, perfectly spaced intervals on the counter. I stood there gawping in silence while he speedily reduced the three-dimensional object to a flat collection of parts. By this point, whether or not the guy should say 'hello' seemed pretty irrelevant. For all his scrawny, mouse-like features, here he was master of his domain.

'I have completed the disassembly,' he says, in this solemn voice. 'Each repair must be brought to completion before the next can take place.'

'Good morning,' he added. Sure, it was closer to lunchtime, but at least he seemed to be getting the hang of the greeting thing.

'Oh . . . morning, Mouse.'

'You were broken. I fixed you.'

Right, I thought, so he's going to say that every time. Seemed like it would get old pretty quick, to be honest, but I decided to roll with it.

Anyway, that's how the Mouse ended up working for us. But it wasn't long until the trouble started.

———

One day I came in to hear Kosaki yelling. When I opened the door, he had the Mouse by the scruff of the neck.

'Oi, cool it!' I shouted. 'What's going on?'

Kosaki was hoisting the guy up by his collar, but he still managed to turn to me and say, in this strained voice:

116

'Good morning. You were broken, and I fixed you.'

There he is, about to take a major beating, and yet he still spouts his usual greeting. I had to laugh.

'The guy bumped into me, and he won't even say sorry!' growled Kosaki.

'Mouse, did you bump into him?' I figured I should at least ask.

'He bumped into me, I'm telling ya!' said Kosaki.

'Shut up, I'm talking to the Mouse. Hey, Mouse, you bump into him?'

'I was advancing forwards. Mr Kosaki impeded my travel.'

'You coulda just gone round me!'

But according to the Mouse's logic, it was Kosaki's fault for getting in the way.

'Mouse,' I explained, 'when you do something like this you have to apologize. You know, "Sorry". "Beg your pardon". That kind of thing.'

'That would be lying.'

It seemed like, to the Mouse, apologizing when he didn't think he'd done anything wrong was the same as lying.

'Come on, Kosaki, you can put him down now. That's just how he is, alright?'

'Sure. But he could at least apologize.'

'Yeah, but like he says, that would be lying,' I said, unable to stop myself smiling again.

For a moment, Kosaki also seemed like he was about to break into a grin. But then his face returned to its usual scowl, and he clicked his tongue in the Mouse's direction. 'You try that again, and you're outta here. Get that into your head, okay?'

'Get it into my head?'

'Yeah. Don't forget.'

'Get what into my head?'

'Urgh . . . never mind.'

Kosaki was fed up by this point, and retreated upstairs. When he'd gone, I turned to the Mouse and gave him some advice.

'Listen, when something like that happens, it's a lot easier to just say sorry, okay? Even if you think it's a lie.'

'But lying is a type of malfunction.'

I never quite knew what was going on in that head of his. Still, it impressed me the way he never backed down, whatever the situation.

It turned out that not apologizing was a bit of a theme with the Mouse. Even when he was clearly the one in the wrong, he refused to say sorry. Then he'd use his weird logic to justify the lack of an apology.

The next day, I got a call from Kosaki. 'Mr Waniguchi, the Mouse is acting up again. You gotta help me here.'

I made my way over to the workshop. From outside,

118

it was immediately clear what the problem was. In the window of the upstairs office, the Mouse had placed an enormous sign on which he'd written, in imposing black lettering: *WE FIX THINGS*. He'd written it by hand, but the characters were so neat and uniform they could have been printed. He'd probably measured them out with a ruler, right down to the millimetre.

The problem was, we weren't supposed to be fixing anything, really. The workshop was just somewhere for us to store stuff; we'd never planned on any actual customers showing up. We hadn't handed out flyers or advertised our presence at all, and the way the place looked, customers weren't exactly going to just wander in.

I walked in to find Kosaki yelling, 'Take it down right now!' Meanwhile, the Mouse was just standing there with this blank look on his face. A snail would have responded faster.

'Good morning,' he said to me.

'Morning.'

'You were broken. I fixed you.' The usual routine.

'Mr Waniguchi, help me out here!' said Kosaki.

'Can't you take it down?'

'He's welded it on somehow!'

Looking around, I noticed that the workshop was full of what looked like even more repair equipment. The Mouse must have brought it in on one of our days off.

Just then, the door to the shop clattered open behind us.

'Hello?'

I casually ducked out of sight – after all, I didn't want any unsavoury rumours about us spreading in the neighbourhood. Hiding behind a pile of junk, I caught a glimpse of our customer. She appeared to be a local housewife, and was holding an electric grill.

'Excuse me, I heard you fix things here?'

'Nah, we don't.' – 'Yes, we do.'

Kosaki and the Mouse replied at exactly the same time. The woman looked startled by their contradictory responses. 'Well, the lady two doors down from me said you fixed something for her. A foot massager, I think it was?'

So this wasn't even our first customer. Kosaki seemed just as surprised as I was, but he must have decided that turning the woman away now would only increase the risk of nasty rumours spreading. His voice suddenly friendly, he announced: 'Ah, yes, we'd be pleased to help!'

I'd heard Kosaki came from a family of grocers. Sure, he'd ditched school at fourteen to become a runner for a gang, and later worked at a host club. But from the way he said these words, there was no doubting his shopkeeping roots. In fact, I found myself thinking he'd make a much better salesman than yakuza grunt.

'This grill's broken. It doesn't heat up properly.'

'I can fix that.' The Mouse spoke with complete assurance, like some hotshot doctor making a diagnosis.

'Wonderful. How long will it take?' asked the woman.

'Forty-eight minutes,' the Mouse shot back.

The woman seemed pretty startled by the level of precision, but she carried on: 'And how much do you think it'll cost, roughly speaking?'

The Mouse fell silent, like he hadn't seen this part coming. Money didn't seem to enter into the guy's equation. Chances were he'd done the foot massager as a freebie.

'One thousand eight hundred yen,' cut in Kosaki. He must have figured that was as much as the woman would cough up to fix the grill instead of just buying a new one. She seemed to think it a fair price, because she nodded, left the grill on the counter, and strolled on out of there.

'Oi, Mouse. You can't go putting signs up without asking Mr Waniguchi here first . . . Hey, listen to me when I'm speaking!'

'Easy now,' I cut in. Then I turned to Kosaki and told him, real quiet: 'We might as well have a few customers. You know, to keep up appearances.'

It'd be a lot more hassle trying to find a replacement for the Mouse if he quit. If we wanted the guy to stick around for the long haul, we'd probably have to let him do his thing every now and then. It was like collecting on a loan – you don't do it all at once, you squeeze it out of them bit by bit.

'But . . .' said Kosaki. The guy didn't want to budge.

'Listen,' I told him, 'it's not like they're going to be pouring through the doors. It'll just be a few locals.'

'If you say so, boss . . .' said Kosaki grumpily, shaking his head and muttering something to himself.

Now, whatever the Mouse was fixing, he'd start by taking the thing apart completely, laying the pieces out on the counter neatly as he went. It was like watching a tape on fast-forward. For some reason, I could never take my eyes off the guy.

When he'd taken it all apart and identified the source of the problem, he'd clean everything, fix whatever needed fixing, and put the whole thing back together in a flash. Logically speaking, all he really needed to do was fix the part that was actually broken, but there was something about this technique of his that just felt *right*, you know?

Watching him fix the grill, I asked him: 'Why'd you bother taking the whole thing apart like that?'

'It's the correct approach.'

When I asked him why it was 'correct', he told me: 'Because it makes everything equal.'

I guessed he meant the balance between all the parts. If you just fixed one part, that could throw the balance of the whole thing off. Even I could see that mixing new and old parts in the same machine might cause some kind of malfunction.

Eventually, he announced: 'I fixed it.'

I looked up at the clock on the wall, did a quick calculation, and realized he'd taken exactly forty-eight minutes. Normally you'd only know how long something would take to repair once you'd opened the thing up and had a look, but the Mouse just seemed to know somehow.

The woman came to collect the grill, and seemed very pleased when she saw that it looked basically brand new – not a hint of grease or anything. She handed over her one thousand eight hundred yen and went home beaming. When I thought about it, most electric shops these days don't bother with repairs – they just tell you you'd be better off buying a new one. I guess people would be pretty happy to have a shop in the neighbourhood that would actually fix things up for them.

———

Maybe it was the sign the Mouse had put up, or maybe it was just word of mouth, but Andromeda Used Goods started seeing a steady trickle of customers. Before long, the Mouse wasn't just fixing the stuff in the warehouse, but all sorts of things that people brought in out of the blue.

Kosaki didn't seem to like explaining things on the Mouse's behalf. Instead, he'd stuck up a price grid, with

'Big', 'Medium' and 'Small' written along the side, and 'Easy', 'Medium' and 'Hard' along the bottom, together with a note that said 'Other Rates Subject to Inquiry'.

One day, I looked out of the office window to see a little girl approaching the shop. She looked about primary school age – in fact, she was probably on the way home from class. I could see what looked like tears on her face. Worrying that this might be out of the Mouse's comfort zone, I hurried downstairs and listened from the crack of the door. It turned out the girl's hamster had died.

'I heard you can fix anything. Does that mean you can fix Coco?'

Great. Now the Mouse was being asked to resurrect the dead.

'I can fix that,' declared the Mouse, in this voice that made it sound definitive. The girl beams and says, 'Wow, really? How long will it take?'

'Eight days.' Seemed he wanted to take his time with this one.

The kid walked off, wiping away her tears. I strolled in like I hadn't heard a thing. The dead hamster was lying there in its cage on the counter. It had this little brown mark on its backside that looked just like the kana character for the sound 'co'. That explained Coco, then.

I picked the cage up and gave it a shake, but the

hamster was well and truly dead. Its body was already rock solid.

'Good morning,' said the Mouse, while I stood there still holding the cage.

'Morning.'

'You were broken. I fixed you.'

There we go.

'Looks like you've finally met your match, Mouse. Did you really have to tell her you could fix it?'

'I can fix it. I need to do research.'

'Research?'

'Yes, research. I haven't fixed a hamster before.' He started making for the door.

I tried stopping him. 'Hey, Mouse, where do you think you're going? You're supposed to be at work!'

But the truth is I was pretty curious where he was going and what this 'research' of his would involve. As far as I knew, fixing dead hamsters wasn't exactly a common procedure.

'Oi, Kosaki!' I called up to the office. 'I'm heading out for a bit with the Mouse.'

Kosaki appeared in the window and gave a sort of weary nod in response. The Mouse began striding towards the river, like he had a specific destination in mind. I was just about to ask where the hell he was taking me when we arrived in front of the large local library. Inside, he walked up to one of the terminals at the counter, searched for the word 'hamster', then printed out the references for what seemed to be every book in the library about the creatures.

Illustrated encyclopaedias, magazines, books on pet-rearing, books on bone structures, picture books, specialist manuals, books which seemed completely irrelevant – one after the other, he retrieved every single item on his list and piled them all on a desk.

While I was still gazing at his tower of books, he'd already opened one of them and began reading it from cover to cover at mind-blowing speed. I didn't have the heart to tell him that it might be quicker to check the contents page for whatever it was he was looking for.

I stood there watching him doing his thing for a while, wondering what in the hell he hoped to gain from it, then went off to find the smoking area, which turned out to be pretty far away. I came back, watched him some more, then went for another smoke break. By the time I got back from my second break, the pile of books had almost completely disappeared.

'So, Mouse, worked out how to fix a dead hamster yet?' I asked him, though of course I wasn't serious.

'Yes, I've ascertained the method.'

'. . . What?'

When he'd carefully returned the remaining books to the

shelves, the Mouse set off back the way we'd come. The guy was basically doing whatever he pleased at this point.

After that, the Mouse stopped going home in the evenings. He just slept on the floor in the workshop instead. His dad kept turning up with this concerned look on his face, bringing him changes of clothes and food. But the Mouse barely ate a bite. Hardly seemed to sleep either – just stayed up all night tinkering with whatever it was that he was making. He even got Kosaki to order him a bunch of weird chemicals with hard-to-pronounce foreign names.

So, it's eight days later. I'm dying to see what this 'hamster repair' looks like.

I open the door to the workshop.

'Good morning,' he says.

'It's afternoon already.'

'You were broken. I fixed you.'

'What about the hamster, then?' I said, joking.

'The repair is complete.'

I looked down at the cage – and couldn't believe my own eyes. There was the hamster, looking very . . . alive. It was sniffing, looking for food, wriggling about, crouching in the corner of the cage – being a cute little hamster, basically.

Looking at the thing, I couldn't help but shudder. He really had fixed the hamster. For a moment I wondered if he'd just bought a replacement, but then I saw the distinctive mark on its backside. No doubt about it – it was the exact same hamster.

You have to be joking, I thought.

When I stuck my hand into the cage and tried grabbing the creature, it just sort of sat there obediently in my grasp.

It was the weight of the thing that gave the game away.

'Mouse . . . I'm not sure this counts as fixing it.'

As I said these words, the little girl turned up. As usual, I slipped out of sight.

'Wow, you fixed her!' I heard her say.

'Your hamster was broken,' said the Mouse. 'I fixed it.'

Overjoyed, the kid picked up the cage and headed home. But something told me this wasn't going to end well.

It wasn't long before I was proven right. The girl's mum turned up – and boy, was she mad.

She burst through the door, shoved the cage onto the counter, and shouted: 'What on *earth* is this?' Her daughter was standing behind her, blubbering away.

'I fixed it,' said the Mouse.

'What do you mean, you *fixed* it? What did you . . . *do* to it?'

'I replaced the inside with mechanisms, tanned the skin, and inserted a—'

The mother looked like she was about to heave. 'What are you *talking* about!'

'I fixed it. It moves the same as before.'

It was true: he'd managed to make the hamster move just like it used to. But that wasn't really the same as 'fixing' it.

'Moves the same? It's an abomination! You owe us a big apology, mister!'

And sure, a heartfelt apology would probably have calmed her down. But this is the Mouse we're talking about. And the Mouse never apologized.

'I fixed it. As you can see, its behaviour is unchanged.'

'Are you kidding me? It isn't . . . alive! Living things eat food! They have . . . warm bodies!'

At this, the Mouse seemed to plunge into thought.

'I will add a digestion function. I could also attach a radiator to generate heat.'

'That's not the point, mister. You tried to con us! I'll sue you! Damage to property, that's what this is!'

Seeing that things were getting a little heated, I decided to make my appearance.

'Hello there,' I said.

The mother flinched visibly when she saw the scar on my cheek.

'I'm sorry, madam. It appears my employee here has done something to upset you?'

When you look like me, the scariest thing you can do is talk politely. I know that from experience.

'You must be rather angry if you're thinking about

129

suing us. We'd like to pay you a visit to apologize. You live nearby, don't you? I suppose you must, if this is your school district. Your daughter has just started school, hasn't she? She's adorable.'

The mother began backing away from me, shielding her child.

'I suppose we could find out where you lived if we waited outside school for her. You know, so we can all come round and tell you just how *sorry* we are.'

'No, there'll be no need for that. We'll be on our way now.'

Once they were outside, the mother began running, half dragging her daughter alongside her.

Meanwhile, there I was with the Mouse and the so-called hamster in its cage. It was sort of cute, in its way – scurrying this way and that, twitching its nose. But I could also see why the kid's mum had flipped like that. There was something about the hamster in front of me that gave even me the creeps.

'Listen, Mouse. You really can't call this "fixing" something, okay?'

'I fixed it. As long as the batteries are periodically replaced, it will continue operating indefinitely.'

'It looks and moves just like a hamster, I'll give you that. But . . . how can I put this – you haven't brought it back to *life*.'

'What is life?'

It took me a minute to wrap my head around that one. See, the hamster was scurrying about in its cage, just like a regular hamster. All those gadgets inside meant that, as far as appearances were concerned, it was no different from a living one. If you didn't know better, you'd swear it was the real deal. What did being 'alive' mean? Was it something to do with having a warm body? Or eating food?

'Mouse, all I can tell you is that this is a dead hamster. Even you know that, right?'

'Yes. The internal organs have stopped functioning. The body has become stiff.'

I was about to say, *So you do get it then!* But then Mouse carried on.

'Which is why I fixed it.'

'Listen. If you had made the organs work again, and the body all warm and soft, then maybe you could claim you'd resurrected the thing. But once something's dead, not even the best doctor in the world can bring it back. No one can.'

'That's why I removed the defunct organs, tanned the hide, and replaced the eyeballs with sensors. I installed a mechanism programmed to move around the cage in various patterns. With proper maintenance it will essentially run for ever. If anything, its functions are an improvement on the original hamster.'

131

'But . . .' I wanted to try and tell the kid what 'life' was, but I couldn't quite find the words. 'Just . . . no more "fixing" dead pets, okay? That's a rule.'

'Why?'

'Because the owners will flip.'

'Why will they flip?'

Good question. It was pretty hard to put into words why the sight of that 'hamster' running around made my skin crawl the way it did. By the time I'd struggled through an explanation and got the Mouse to promise not to fix dead animals, I was exhausted.

I stood there staring at the hamster, wondering if the Mouse had really understood. The hamster was just sitting there in the corner of the cage, its nose twitching away.

———

After that incident, I thought we might not see any more customers, but Andromeda Used Goods remained surprisingly popular with the locals. Luckily, though, nobody else asked us to fix their hamster.

For some reason, I found myself spending all day at the office. Kosaki must have wondered why I kept turning up, but in the end he just told me he was busy doing the accounts and carried on clicking away at the computer. Meanwhile, I spent all my time watching the Mouse through the window in the floor. The guy had become a permanent fixture in the workshop – beavering away all day like he'd been there for decades, and would be for many more.

As ever, he worked at insane speed. It amazed me how he never seemed to get confused about what he was doing, but that was just how he was, I guess. The Mouse had his own way of doing things, and it was different from our own. Although, when I thought about it, what we called normal probably wasn't very normal either. Ever since the Mouse had turned up, I'd started thinking about all sorts of things I'd never thought about before. Probably because he wasn't the kind of person I'd ever been around before. Sure, there was room for all sorts in our organization – number crunchers, tough guys, crooked lawyers. But the Mouse was in a genre all of his own.

One day, another little kid turned up. Come on, I thought – we're a repair shop, not a counselling service.

He was probably in the upper years of primary school, but his skin was darker than your average kid. Maybe he played a lot of sports or something. There was something unusual about his features, too. He had one of the leather backpacks that primary school kids always carried, but there was something different about the guy.

I made my way downstairs, thinking I'd just tell him this wasn't a place for kids and send him home. But then I walked into the workshop and saw he was clutching something in his hands. The kid's fists were clenched so tight they were shaking. He looked like he was trying his hardest not to cry.

Then I heard him speak, and it all made sense.

'Fix – fixing. Fixing, please. Thank you.'

From the way he spoke, it was pretty clear the kid wasn't Japanese. He brushed the tears from his eyes, then produced a load of paper scraps and placed them onto the counter.

His little backpack was all battered, and on top of that, there were all these shoe prints on it. Looking closer, I could see them on his clothes too. Judging from the water dripping from his backpack, its contents must have been dunked in a toilet or something.

On the counter, strewn about like the pieces of a jigsaw puzzle, were the remains of a photo.

It wasn't hard to guess what had happened. Kids that age can be brutal. They don't know better. If you don't blend in or play along, you're fair game.

'Yes, I can fix that,' says the Mouse.

Now, I'm thinking to myself: *Hang on, you're restoring photos now? I thought you were more of a gadget guy.* But the Mouse seemed to have all the bases covered.

The kid says: 'Take how long?'

'Six days,' replies the Mouse.

Then I open the door and the Mouse looks over at me.

'Good morning,' says the Mouse.

134

'Hi.'

'You were broken. I fixed you.'

With the usual greeting out the way, I turn to our customer. 'You okay, kid? What's your name?'

'Tien. Nguyen Minh Tien.'

'Where you from?'

'Vietnam.'

'You got family here?'

'Father here. Mother, sister live in Nha Trang.'

Unable to help myself, I brushed some of the mud off his uniform. Tien flinched away from my hand like a kitten raising its hackles.

'Did you tell the teacher?' I asked.

If the kid's Japanese was this bad, chances were his dad didn't speak a word. He probably didn't have anyone he could turn to for help. If he didn't have such a fierce look in his eyes, the bullies might have got bored and moved on to someone else. But Tien's eyes burned like coals. Yeah, he made a good target.

'Six days. Got it?' I said, showing him six fingers. 'Six days, come back.'

'Six days, come back,' repeated the kid. Then he bowed and left.

Wondering what kind of photo could matter so much to him, I looked back at the counter to see that the Mouse had almost finished piecing it back together.

'Oh,' I groaned. It was a family portrait. Looked like a birthday party or something.

The kid must have treasured it. Looked at it every day. It probably never left his side. And the bullies knew that, and that's why they'd done this. They'd shredded it into dozens of pieces, but the kid had retrieved every last one.

Now, sure, I've done my fair share of debt-collecting. But when it comes to bullying, there's a certain line you just don't cross. I didn't know who these brats were, but if this was their idea of a good time, they must be pretty messed up inside.

Punch someone and the bruise goes away eventually. But if you destroy something that means the world to them, there's no healing that wound.

'Mouse, reckon you can fix this?'

'Yes, I can fix it.'

Same response as always.

'Well, make a good job of it, alright?'

He told me he was off to the library again. I was curious what he was planning, so I went along with him. Just like before, he gathered this huge pile of books.

I thought he might start brushing up on his computer skills, but I was wrong. I'd assumed that by 'repairing' the photo, he just meant scanning all the pieces, fiddling with them on the computer, and printing out a fresh copy. It turned out he had something else in mind.

When the Mouse said he was going to fix something, he didn't just mean he was going to print out a new one or whatever. He meant he was going to fix it.

Next, he hauled this giant microscope into the workshop. It turned out he was planning to manually join up all the torn edges of the photo. We're talking micromillimetres here. I just didn't get it – I mean, wouldn't the frayed parts be just as visible once he'd joined them up?

When I asked him about that, he turned round and started reeling off this long explanation – you know, like he was reading it straight from a book. Something about how photographic paper had three colour layers which combined to – well, anyway, at some point I stopped him and said: 'Alright, alright, I get the picture.'

Basically, he wanted to recolour the photo himself. Still, even when he'd glued it together perfectly and let it dry off, it was still all white and frayed where it had been torn. Just like I'd warned him. If he manually coloured those parts in, wouldn't that just make them stand out even more? But, as usual, the Mouse managed to surprise me.

The guy gets out what looks like a paintbrush, except it has just a single bristle, finer than a needle.

'The hell is that, Mouse?' I ask him.

'A colour restoration tool,' he replies, like it's obvious. He starts mixing up colours on a palette. Then he peers through the microscope, and makes a single point with the brush.

I couldn't quite believe it, but it seemed he was going to use that single bristle to create a whole mosaic of dots, one by one. The guy sat there from morning until the night, peering through the microscope, making his tiny marks.

———

Still, no matter how much time and effort the Mouse put into restoring the photograph, that wasn't going to stop the bullies from tearing it up again. I decided to park my Lexus not far from the school and see what I could observe.

What I saw wasn't pretty. What really got under my skin was the way everyone just ignored it. Even the teachers – they just strolled on by like they didn't see a thing. So I started the car up nice and quiet and followed Tien. He was trying to walk home, but these three guys kept throwing a ball at the kid's head and shoving him. Whenever he tried to fight back, two of them would restrain him while the other booted him in the stomach. They were big guys, probably a couple of years above him. He had no chance. Their sick game wasn't over yet, either. When they were sure no one was looking, they grabbed his backpack and used it to lure him down to the riverside. These kids were basically professionals.

Soon the contents of the backpack were littered all over the ground, and they started chucking all his books and stuff right into the river. They all hooted with laughter at the sight of the books floating around on the river. But Tien still wasn't crying. He was gritting his teeth, trying to get through it. I guess he'd realized it was pointless trying to resist, or maybe he didn't want to get too close to the river – in any case, he just grabbed his empty backpack and set off home.

Part of me thought I should stay out of it. I mean, the kid was going to have to toughen up at some point if he wanted to survive. But then it'd be a real pain if he started coming in and asking us to fix his exercise books. Ever since Tien had come into the shop, the Mouse had done nothing but work on the photo, even if it meant slacking off on the rest of his work.

So in the end, I went and stood right behind the three kids. They were still gripping their sides with laughter.

'What's so funny? Go on, let me in on the secret.'

They turned around with these gormless looks on their faces – and what do they see? My nice, friendly smile. That, and the blade scar on my left cheek. One of them tried to run, so I grabbed him by the scruff of his neck.

'Oh, this *does* look like fun. Racing pencil cases down the river, are we?'

Just as the kids tried to force a laugh, I turned all serious.

'Just *having fun*, were you?'

They nodded.

'Yeah, I'll show you fun.'

Then, one by one, I jammed my foot into their bellies, sending them toppling backwards into the river. It being the middle of winter, I imagine it wasn't exactly pleasant in there.

'No getting out 'til you've fished all that stuff out, okay? I don't want a single pencil left behind.'

I stood there smoking on the bank while I waited. Shivering, the kids brought the pencil case and exercise books and laid them at my feet.

'Is that everything?'

They nodded, their teeth chattering. Then I booted all three of them back into the river.

'I don't think it is, you know.'

'But it is!'

'Yeah? I sort of feel like it isn't.'

After I pushed them in a couple more times, they started crying, so I decided to leave it there. After my good deed, the sky seemed bluer, somehow. And my cigarette tasted nicer.

———•———

At this point in his story, Waniguchi stopped and had a good stretch. Seen from the pedestrian bridge, the crowds in front of the station seemed endless. Two parents and their child walked past carrying a cake box. Probably on their way home to enjoy Christmas together, he thought.

He and Hirasaka would have to get going soon if they wanted to take that photo.

In front of a fast-food restaurant, three employees in Santa hats were standing by some tables and enthusiastically promoting a special Christmas menu. Somewhere, 'Jingle Bells' was playing. It looked like the station itself was going to light up in the shape of a Christmas tree when evening came.

'What did you do with the pencil case afterwards?' asked Hirasaka, clearly still intrigued by Waniguchi's story. 'Did you wash it and give it back to him or something?'

'It was covered in sludge. I didn't want to touch it, so I just left it there. This might surprise you, but I'm sort of a clean freak.'

Hirasaka winced, then resumed his usual mild expression.

A moment later, he gave Waniguchi a look as if to suggest they get going, and began gathering up the rubbish from their picnic.

'Why bother cleaning up? None of these people can even see it, right?'

'True. But there's just something about leaving it here that bothers me,' replied Hirasaka, emptying the rubbish into a nearby bin.

They began wandering in the direction of the nearby primary school. As they approached a park, they began to hear the excited yelps of children. It looked like some kind of relay race was taking place. Two nursery school teachers – one in an apron, older and experienced-looking, and one in a tracksuit who looked more like a new recruit – were cheering the kids on. One of the teachers shouted, *Come on!* in a voice so deafening they found themselves laughing. The kids ran around and around, their little cheeks red with exertion. On the last lap the teachers themselves joined in the race. Good for them, thought Waniguchi. Watching the new recruit desperately trying to catch up with her senior, the kids were all screaming, *Come on, Miss Michi!* Waniguchi carried on walking, but Hirasaka had stopped and was gazing at the scene. The guy must have a soft spot for kids, thought Waniguchi.

He found himself wondering what it was going to feel like to see his past self. Presumably, right now, the 'other' Waniguchi was still very much alive and kicking.

They reached the gates of the primary school, where they waited until the bell rang, signalling the end of the school day. As he stood there absent-mindedly watching the kids file out of the gates, thinking to himself that their backpacks were much more colourful these days, out walked a kid with a slightly darker face than the others. It was Tien. This was only a day after the incident at the river, which explained why he was looking around so cautiously. He seemed almost surprised that no one had accosted him yet. It looked like being repeatedly dunked in a wintry river had taught the bullies a lesson. Maybe they'd caught colds and taken the day off school.

He wondered how they'd explained their sopping wet clothes to their parents. It looked like they hadn't kicked up a fuss about it, in any case. Maybe deep down, they knew they'd been in the wrong.

Tien began walking home, frequently looking over his shoulder. Then he suddenly stopped short. There they were, approaching the crossroads. The bullies.

'You see 'em?' said Waniguchi, pointing them out to Hirasaka. 'Look at the mugs on 'em. Real nasty types, huh?'

One of them, wearing a loose-fitting uniform, was clearly the ringleader. He swaggered along, followed closely by his two lackeys.

When they saw Tien, the three boys averted their gaze, muttered briefly to each other, then went on their way. Tien stared at them, still rooted to the spot. He looked confused, but relieved.

This wouldn't be the end of it. Sure, he'd survive just fine in Japan. But getting to grips with the language, learning how to blend in, building genuine friendships – he still had plenty of mountains to climb. For little Tien, the battle had only just begun.

But for today, at least, you can breathe easy, thought Waniguchi.

They followed Tien. As Andromeda Used Goods came into view, his pace quickened. By the time he pushed the door open, he was practically sprinting. It was Christmas last year, when things at the workshop had been relatively normal.

Waniguchi began to feel quite peculiar. There, in front of him, was his past self. Sitting there, very much alive, leaning back self-importantly with his legs crossed. The Mouse, meanwhile, was tinkering away at something as usual.

He tried calling out to himself. 'Oi, me! Hey! Listen up!'

But the living Waniguchi just carried on sitting there, oblivious to his every word.

'I'm sorry,' said Hirasaka. 'Here in the past, no one can see us. We can't talk to them, or attempt to change our own destiny. All we can do is take that photo.'

Waniguchi snorted slightly and folded his arms. 'So I can't tell this guy he'd better watch his back?'

'That's right. Changing someone's destiny is strictly forbidden. Not that it's even possible . . .'

Just then, Tien began to speak.

'Hello,' he said in his usual lilting accent. The Mouse looked up. Waniguchi's past self was watching discreetly from a distance, too. The Mouse produced the photograph and laid it on the counter.

'The photo was broken. I fixed it.'

Tien gave a little gasp, then reached out and stroked the photo. Tears started rolling down his cheeks.

'This guy fixed it using a microscope,' said the living Waniguchi to Tien, jerking his chin in the direction of the instrument. 'Recoloured it by hand. Then he applied a coating of – well, some kind of chemical. See how it's all nice and smooth again?'

Tien was beaming through his tears. Despite how long the job had taken, they charged him the lowest fee on the board. He paid almost entirely with loose change.

'Hey, mister,' murmured Waniguchi, 'pass me that Leica, would ya?'

Hirasaka got out an exposure meter and measured the light. Then, after finding a good spot from which to take the photo, he peered through the viewfinder of the Leica, adjusted a few dials, and finally handed it over.

Waniguchi held the camera up to his eye. There they were, all framed in the shot. Tien, his face screwed up so that you couldn't tell if he was crying or laughing, the Mouse standing there silently with his usual blank expression, and . . . Waniguchi himself, looking just the way he always had. A pretty weird scene, all told. But for some reason, he liked it.

He pressed the shutter, and felt it gently click.

Thanking them over and over again, Tien made his way out of the shop.

The living Waniguchi turned to the Mouse. 'Giving it back to him today of all days – that your idea of a Christmas present, huh?' But the Mouse simply began reciting the time required for each of the processes involved in the repair.

'Alright, alright,' grinned Waniguchi. 'I get it.'

Tien reappeared again soon afterwards. In his outstretched hand was a square log of glutinous rice wrapped in leaves of some kind. It tasted like nothing they'd ever eaten.

———

Waniguchi blinked – and found himself back in the photo studio.

'Welcome back,' said Hirasaka. 'Shall I make some coffee?'

It felt like they'd returned from a very long journey.

'Two sugars. With a splash of whiskey, too.'

He heard the faint sound of coffee beans being ground, and a pleasant aroma drifted into the room.

'A few months after that, I got stabbed in the back.'

The grinding stopped.

'A single jab in my back, and that was it. Don't know who, though. Plenty of people had grudges against me. What cheesed me off was that the Mouse was just arriving at work as it happened. The guy must have really freaked out at the sight of me all covered in blood.'

Waniguchi had begun sorting through the photos. When the coffee was ready, Hirasaka brought it through.

'I'll just be in the darkroom, developing your photo,' he said, setting the mug down on the table. 'Would you like to see how it's done?'

Waniguchi imagined the two of them crammed into a stuffy darkroom together.

'Nah, I'll leave that up to you. But . . . do it right, okay?'

'Certainly,' smiled Hirasaka. 'You can count on me.'

As he leafed through his forty-seven years' worth of photos, Waniguchi began to realize that his life had been pretty eventful, after all. He'd assumed choosing one for each year would be a breeze, but now found himself weighing his options at length, gazing intently at each photo. His first marriage, and the divorce that came soon after. The kid he never saw any more. His second marriage. The day he got out of prison . . .

In the end, the task took him a long time – and a lot of concentration.

'Ah, excellent work,' said Hirasaka, his voice filling with appreciation as he surveyed Waniguchi's final selection. 'And here's the one you took earlier.'

He produced the freshly developed photograph and, handling it as carefully as he would a newborn child, presented it to Waniguchi.

Right, thought Waniguchi, let's see what that Elmar thing is capable of.

The photo was black and white. You're kidding, he thought. It's not even colour?

The three-dimensional scene in the workshop had been reduced to the flat, glossy surface of the photo. But the more he looked, the more he began to notice something very special about the print. It was like the camera had somehow peeled off a single layer of reality and brought it back with them. That single tear that was threatening to drop from Tien's half-smiling, half-blubbering cheeks – it seemed so *real*. The same went for the Mouse's scrawny figure and blank expression or, further back, his own face. Captured in these soft grey tones, every element of the photo, down to the wrinkles in their clothes, seemed perfectly in balance, like a carefully composed shot in a classic film.

In other words, it was a pretty decent photograph.

'Looks like my camera skills aren't too shabby, huh?' said Waniguchi, handing back the print.

Hirasaka smiled. 'Oh, absolutely. It's exactly the finishing touch your lantern needs.' With that, he disappeared back into his workshop.

While he waited for Hirasaka to finish whatever it was he was working on, Waniguchi filled a glass with ice, poured himself some whiskey, gave it a stir with his finger, then began gulping it down. Just then, he noticed the framed photo of Hirasaka.

Wow, mister, he thought. Didn't know you were the narcissistic type.

But then he remembered Hirasaka saying that he had no memories – and that his only real possession was a photo of himself, about which he knew nothing.

This must be the photo. Gazing at it, Waniguchi decided to try playing the detective. He had watched enough crime dramas.

Judging from the backdrop, the photo had been taken in some kind of forest. In it, Hirasaka was smiling vaguely. He looked happy.

When, a while later, Hirasaka came to find him, Waniguchi turned around with a serious expression and declared the findings of his investigation.

'See that smile on your face? That's the smile of someone who's just bought a patch of land. Mister, in your former life, you were a shiitake farmer.'

'A shiitake farmer . . .?'

'You look like someone who enjoys shiitake mushrooms. This smile of yours – it looks to me like you've just had a bite of one of them, and you loved it.'

'I see.' Hirasaka looked unconvinced.

'I guess what I'm trying to say is, I reckon you were a decent guy.'

They stared at the photo for a while longer.

'Well, everything's ready,' said Hirasaka. 'This way, please.'

Waniguchi followed him into the white room opposite and settled himself on the sofa, crossing his arms and legs. Everything felt soft and warm.

On the other side of the room, the lantern was already lit, casting an array of colours onto the floor.

'Once the lantern starts spinning, please keep your eyes on it until it comes to a halt. By the time that happens, you'll be on your way.'

Lit from behind, each of his photos seemed to emit its own glow.

'Right then. Here we go,' said Hirasaka, reaching towards the lantern.

The lantern began to turn.

I guess anyone's life would look pretty spinning around like this, thought Waniguchi to himself. Even that of some deadbeat who got himself stabbed in the back.

'Not much of a life, was it . . .?' he murmured.

He watched as the chubby little one-year-old in the first photo turned two, and then three, and then four, getting taller all the time. He thought about his mother, who had abandoned him around then. Was she still alive, he wondered? Had she seen his death on the news and recognized him somehow? He looked pretty different these days, after all, and the television station wouldn't have bothered to try and show him in a good light. In fact, they'd probably used the nastiest photo of him they could find.

All the choices he'd made, the decisions he'd made at each of life's crossroads – they were what led him to that grisly end, he thought.

Now he was looking at a photo of himself as a nine-year-old. He was standing at the top of a jungle gym, staring off into the distance.

If I'd only chosen another path back then, he thought. If I'd only made a few different choices. For a start, not punching that idiot of a teacher back in school . . .

Though, even if I got to do the whole thing over, I'd probably still end up punching him. Might even have kicked him a couple of times for good measure. Yeah, I definitely would have. Maybe even a headbutt. I really couldn't stand the guy.

Anyway, the phrase 'if only' meant nothing in life. He was the product of his choices, and that was all there was to it.

Still. If only . . .

'You know, if I get reincarnated, I think I might like to run a thrift shop. Might not be the most exciting life, but still.'

Hirasaka smiled gently in response.

The photos began to take on a vague, hazy appearance. Their colours seemed to fade. Then he came to the final photo, in black and white. The last photo he'd ever taken – and he'd taken it with a scrawny-looking guy and a teary-eyed kid. Bit depressing. Or maybe, he thought, it would do just fine.

'Here we go,' murmured Waniguchi.

The lantern slowed, and the light seemed to intensify. As he closed his eyes, he felt his consciousness gradually blurring, like he was falling asleep.

And then the lantern came to a halt.

———•———

By now the room was bathed in white light. Waniguchi's body began to fade, like it was being slowly absorbed by the dazzle. By the time the room had returned to its normal brightness, he was nowhere to be seen.

Hirasaka stood there, alone again in the room. He had turned on a small lamp and was filling out a form. Standing in front of the lantern, he found his thoughts wandering.

Waniguchi's lantern was still emitting a bluish glow onto the floor. On the side facing him was that black-and-white photo. Waniguchi's last photo – the one he'd taken with the Mouse and Tien. Standing there in the photo, the Mouse really did look like, well, a mouse.

Hirasaka found himself hoping that, in some distant future, the day would come when those two would run a thrift shop together.

Noticing something in his pocket, he took it out and saw that it was the snack Waniguchi had shoved in there. Hirasaka had forgotten all about it. *A little treat to take back with you*, Waniguchi had said. Looking closer, he saw that they were chocolates. On the packet were the words 'Merry Christmas'. Hirasaka chuckled at Waniguchi's bizarre show of kindness.

He returned to his paperwork. Standing in front of the stationary lantern, he recalled everything Waniguchi had told him, copying it down on the form. The scratch of his pen filled the otherwise silent room.

Yama the delivery man would be here again soon. In the same good mood as always, no doubt. A spring in his step. Maybe he should invite him in for a cup of tea – it had been a while since they'd done that. Right now, for some reason, he felt like having a nice long chat with someone.

———•———

Waniguchi felt himself falling.

Then, all of a sudden, he was standing by Kosaki's bedside.

What the . . .

Kosaki, of all people?

So this was what it felt like to come back and haunt someone.

Man, this room is a mess. Would it hurt the guy to tidy it from time to time? Kosaki's bedding was in dire need of changing, and the room was strewn with empty instant ramen cups and trashy convenience store manga. Kosaki was sprawled on his bed, his mouth half open as he slept.

Waniguchi gave him a sudden hard kick. He was relieved to feel his foot actually make contact.

'Oi, rise and shine!'

'What the – Mr Waniguchi? But you already . . . in the hospital . . . Come on, please don't haunt me! . . . Erm . . . Begone, evil spirit!' Kosaki began gesturing towards the door. 'Heaven's that way!'

'Who you calling an evil spirit, eh?'

This time, he tried standing on Kosaki's belly. He could feel that too. He started singing to himself as hopped on and off Kosaki like a footstool.

'See, there's something I should tell you before I go!'

Kosaki was gasping for breath at his feet.

'Keep looking after the Mouse at the shop, okay? Don't

even think about firing him for some dumb reason. If you do, I'll come back and haunt you every damn day. Got that into your thick skull?'

He leaned down towards Kosaki, who wheezed as he tried to crawl away.

'Okay, I get it! I'll look after the guy!'

Waniguchi rolled his eyes in as ghoul-like a manner as he could muster, raising his arms menacingly for extra spookiness.

'You don't want one of my curses on you, I can tell you! You won't be able to open your rice cooker or turn your shower on without my spirit coming out to haunt you.'

'Okay, okay!' shouted Kosaki, curling up defensively under his duvet.

———

Then, in a flash, Waniguchi found himself standing in front of Andromeda Used Goods. The 'We Fix Things' sign was still prominently displayed in the window.

He walked in to find the counter littered with pieces of paper covered with incredibly complex formulas and diagrams. Normally nothing was even a millimetre out of place in the workshop; now, it was a mess. It looked like the Mouse was in the middle of one of his intense repair jobs.

True to his usual routine during such periods, the Mouse had rolled out a thin mat on one of the few available patches of floor, and was sleeping on top of it, his body forming a perfectly straight line.

'Oi, Mouse,' he said, shaking him slightly. The Mouse opened his eyes. He didn't look well. His cheeks were sunken and his face haggard, giving him an even more rodent-like appearance than usual. He rose immediately to his feet.

'Good morning,' he said, looking around. The fact that it was still dark seemed to confuse him slightly. 'You were broken . . .'

Waniguchi stood there, waiting for him to finish his sentence with the customary 'I fixed you'. But it never came.

'I'm sorry,' said the Mouse.

Hearing those words from the kid's mouth came as a huge shock to Waniguchi. He'd never apologized for anything, no matter how many times he'd told him to. And yet there it was – he was sorry.

'What's wrong with you, Mouse?' he asked with a nervous chuckle. 'Did you eat something funny?'

'You were broken.' said the Mouse, looking right at him. 'And I couldn't fix you.'

The kid didn't move a muscle as he spoke. Like he was standing to attention.

'I conducted as much research as possible. But I couldn't fix you.'

There was a long silence before the Mouse spoke again.

'I wanted to fix you.'

———•———

Kosaki woke with a start. His room felt stiflingly hot.

'What a weird dream . . .'

Mr Waniguchi, who had died the day before, had come back to haunt him in his sleep. He'd trampled all over him, threatening to put a curse on him if he fired the Mouse or didn't look after him properly. As Kosaki got up, every joint in his body squealed with pain. His belly was even faintly bruised where Mr Waniguchi's boots had made contact. He scrabbled about for his wallet, then rushed to the convenience store to buy some salt. He'd need it if he was going to cleanse the evil spirit from his apartment.

'Don't you have any big packs?' he asked the clerk. But it seemed those were out of stock, so instead he bought five of the smaller bottles, which actually turned out to have garlic mixed in. Still, he told himself, salt was salt.

When he told people about the visit from Mr Waniguchi's vengeful spirit, they just laughed. But Kosaki knew what he'd seen. He started carrying one of the little bottles of salt with him wherever he went, ready to calmly send his former boss on his way to the afterlife if he showed up again.

Meanwhile, the Mouse was still working at the workshop. Even after Mr Waniguchi's death, he carried on beavering away with his repairs. Kosaki really didn't get the guy.

He wasn't sure what sort of rumours had spread about Andromeda Used Goods, but a steady trickle of customers still passed through its doors every day.

Today, the Mouse had retrieved the hamster he had once 'fixed', and appeared to be tinkering with it again.

'What you doing this time? You going to stick a turbo booster on there or something?'

But instead of replying, the Mouse simply removed the batteries. Then, cradling the hamster in his arms, he took it outside. Unable to contain his curiosity, Kosaki followed him.

The Mouse strode purposefully towards the river, where he laid the hamster gently down on the bank. After pulling up the grass, he used a nearby stick to begin digging away at the ground. The earth was so hard that at first he made hardly any progress, but eventually he seemed to reach a looser layer of soil.

Grabbing a shard from a nearby broken flowerpot, Kosaki started helping the Mouse to dig.

After they'd buried the hamster, they stood there and,

not knowing what else to do, pressed their palms together in prayer.

The smell of freshly dug earth lingered in the air, while a dry wind rustled in the grass. Up on the embankment, joggers passed briskly by. Looking up, Kosaki saw an aeroplane carving a long white trail across the sky. He glanced sideways and saw that the Mouse was looking up, too.

For a while longer, they carried on gazing at the trail in the sky, until it faded entirely into the blue.

Chapter Three

Mitsuru and the Last Photo

Footsteps were approaching the studio. If they were notes on a musical score, you'd call it a staccato rhythm. Maybe even 'jaunty'.

Then came a jolly series of knocks. *Rat-tat, rat-a-tat-tat.*

'Delivery for you, Mr Hirasaka!'

The same old voice. Marvelling, as always, at Yama's ability to be so cheerful about his endlessly repetitive job, Hirasaka opened the door.

Outside stood the delivery man, his cap facing backwards as usual. Today, though, his trolley was nowhere to be seen.

'Today's guest,' he said, holding out a thin envelope.

So that was why he hadn't brought the trolley. If the

number of photos was this small, his 'guest' was probably still a child. Hirasaka signed for the delivery.

'There *are* a few photos,' said Yama, 'but you don't have to actually do anything this time. Just sit there and drink some tea together. She'll be gone again before you know it.'

Hirasaka was startled, until he recalled similar cases from the past. Guests who ended up returning to life. It wasn't frequent, but it happened.

'Oh, right. That's good. I mean, this is a child we're talking about, right? I'm glad to hear her life isn't quite over yet . . .'

But even as he said this, he couldn't fail to notice the way the colour drained from Yama's face.

'Can I see her file?' he asked.

Now that he thought about it, Yama usually cracked all sorts of jokes while he was handing over the file. This time, though, he'd tucked it under his arm without opening it, and even now that Hirasaka had asked to see it, he was still just standing there. This had never happened before.

'Show me the file.'

'The thing is, Mr Hirasaka, this kid has a real tough time of it. She returns to life for a while, but she dies again soon afterwards. I'd say you're better off not knowing the details. Why don't you just make her a cup of tea, and—'

'Show me!'

As Yama reluctantly handed the file over, he noticed the red sticker. So the kid's death had been caused by human hands. He began reading.

'Seriously, Mr Hirasaka,' Yama insisted, 'there's nothing you can do. We're not allowed to change people's destinies, and there'd be hell to pay if we did. Anyway, you're just her guide. Everything has already been decided.'

'. . . I know.'

'Just make her that cup of tea, okay?'

With these words, Yama took his leave.

———

Hirasaka began to sense a presence in the room. Within moments the child had appeared, lying on the sofa.

So, this was his guest.

She was still very young. Her hair was cropped short, like it had been roughly shorn with a razor. Her body was terribly thin, and her face was screwed up like she was having a bad dream. Underneath an old fleece, he could see a T-shirt with superheroes on it. Her legs were poking out from a pair of black shorts. She seemed fast asleep.

Hirasaka silently slipped the photos out of the envelope and laid them out carefully on the reception counter.

Looking at the photos from her short life, his hands froze. He wasn't sure how long he stood there. Eventually, he slowly returned the photos to the envelope and turned towards the sleeping child.

She must have sensed something, because just then her eyes snapped open. Still blinking away her sleep, she met his gaze.

'. . . Miss Yamada. Welcome.'

As he'd expected, the girl was staring at him distrustfully. Then she covered her face with her arms and huddled into herself on the sofa, as if frightened.

'You see, Miss Yamada, I've been waiting for you. Coming here was . . . well, let's say it was your destiny.'

She stared fearfully back at him, completely motionless.

'Your first name's Mitsuru, isn't it? Can I call you that?'

She gave a barely perceptible nod.

'Well, Mitsuru, I wonder what you fancy? I've got plenty of cake, and lots of tasty drinks, too, if you'd like. See, this is my photo studio. Do you want to come on through to the next room?'

Mitsuru's shoulders trembled. She shook her head. Waking up in a place like this all of a sudden must have been quite the shock. He was going to have to tell her the truth.

'The thing is, Mitsuru, you're . . . dead. You're on your way to heaven right now.'

A slight flush seemed to come to Mitsuru's cheeks.

'This photo studio is a sort of rest stop along the way.

Everyone who dies turns up here. There's nothing to worry about any more, Mitsuru. I'm just here to show you the way.'

'I'm . . . dead?' she asked, in the faintest of voices. She stared down at her hands.

'Unfortunately, yes.'

Mitsuru silently hung her head.

'You've still got a bit of time left. How about we go on a little adventure?'

She shook her head.

'We could go to the park, have some chocolate. Play on the swings, throw a ball around, maybe eat some baked sweet potato. It'll be fun, I promise!'

At the mention of chocolate, Mitsuru twitched very slightly.

'Do you like ice cream?'

Mitsuru's eyes darted left and right, as if she wasn't sure what to say.

'Don't worry – guiding people like this is my job. We can even travel back in time if you like. With a camera.'

He opened the door to the equipment room. Mitsuru seemed to hesitate some more, then gave a decisive nod.

'A little trip together – it'll be great. Just wait a moment while I grab us a camera, okay?'

A few moments later, he returned with the camera. It was one a particularly chatty visitor had recommended.

Out of all the cameras in the equipment room, this was the one he felt most comfortable using.

'This here is a Nikon F3. It's a wonderful bit of kit.'

Mitsuru glanced away, as though completely uninterested in the camera.

'Let's get going, then. Stand here next to me, okay?'

Still keeping a wary distance, Mitsuru stood alongside him in front of the door.

The date Hirasaka had chosen, after looking at Mitsuru's last photos, was the sixteenth of March.

————— • —————

The floor seemed to shift beneath their feet. Now they were outside, on a slope. Hirasaka and Mitsuru were standing by the side of a two-lane road in the countryside.

The day was only just dawning. Through a grove of trees, Hirasaka could see the sunlight just starting to catch the ridge of a nearby mountain.

The sudden change of scene must have frightened Mitsuru. She shuddered and turned away from him, as though about to run off down the slope.

'Hey, don't worry! A short way down this mountain there's a bus stop. We can jump on a bus there. We'll find somewhere nice to play, I promise!'

He began walking. After a while, Mitsuru began trudging

along behind. They weren't far from her house, and she might even have been familiar with this road. But she still seemed a little uncertain about all this. In the end, though, it seemed she'd decided that she had no other option.

They walked down the mountain road, hugging the crash barrier around a series of bends, until eventually they emerged into a valley filled with rice fields and a scattering of houses. A bus stop came into view. It was a shed-like structure, with a rudimentary wooden roof for shelter. Inside was a wooden bench. According to the timetable on the wall, there were only two buses an hour. Hirasaka and Mitsuru sat down at opposite ends of the bench.

The early-morning silence was broken by the distant cry of a bird, though Hirasaka couldn't tell what kind.

A boy carrying a bulky sports bag appeared and sat on the space between them on the bench. He looked like he must be on the school baseball team, and kept yawning.

Finally the bus arrived, and the three of them climbed on board. Mitsuru sat right at the back.

Hirasaka relaxed into his own seat. With countryside buses like this, it could be a long while between stops. At one of them, a family boarded the bus: a little boy, who sat happily on his father's lap, and his mother, in whose bag he glimpsed a roll-up mat, a flask, and various bento boxes. She was also carrying a hefty camera. Maybe they were planning on taking a family portrait.

The bus carried on down the road, and the scenery became flatter. When the driver announced the bus stop for the park, Hirasaka indicated to Mitsuru at the back that they should get off. They followed the family off the bus.

With winter retreating and spring already on its way, the sun felt warm on their faces.

'Mitsuru, see that convenience store over there? I'll buy you whatever you want.' At these words, her expression seemed to brighten ever so slightly.

Inside, Mitsuru's eyes began darting from shelf to shelf. When a customer came walking towards her and passed right through her body, she gave a little yelp of surprise.

'No one here can see or hear us, Mitsuru. No one at all. So don't worry – you're quite safe.'

Mitsuru began poking doubtfully at her own belly.

'Have you ever seen people leaving fruits and snacks at graves – you know, for spirits to eat? Well, there's a reason why they do that. Go on, point at anything you want.'

At first she seemed hesitant. But when he told her not to worry about the price, and repeated that she could have whatever she wanted, she began pointing at various items on the shelves. Each time, he'd focus on the item in question – a packet of popcorn, say, or marshmallows – and slowly remove it from the shelf. When he did so, the product appeared to split into two. Mitsuru seemed quite amazed by this magic trick.

When they were done, Mitsuru stared at the counter, as if concerned about how they were going to pay. For the sake of appearances, Hirasaka reassured her that he had this covered, too. Turning to the clerk at the counter who was looking the other way, he pretended to put down some money and said, 'Here you go.'

At the park, they tucked into the treats from the convenience store. Judging from how she ate, Mitsuru must have been very hungry.

There were all sorts of play equipment in the park, which was bustling with children and their parents. Mitsuru didn't seem to know what to do, so Hirasaka tried showing her how to play. He sat her on the swing and gave her a gentle push from behind. They went down the long, winding slide together, and she cried out with excitement when they picked up speed. There was a pond, so he showed her how to skim stones. After a while, she became so engrossed in playing that he left her to it. He watched her making her way around the park, hopping across the stepping stones in the pond, straining to reach the gymnastic rings hanging from a bar . . .

Spotting a trail that led to the top of the small mountain nearby, he asked her if she felt like a walk.

'What do you reckon? I bet the view's nice from up there.'

According to the sign, it was twenty minutes each way – perfect for a short hike.

The trail was surrounded by forest, and its stone steps were blanketed with fallen leaves. As they climbed, the excited voices from the park faded, and soon all they could hear was the gentle crunch of their feet on the leaves. The air was pristine.

Glancing up, Hirasaka could see several orb-like bunches of leaves among the otherwise bare branches.

'See those leaves, Mitsuru?' She looked up. 'That's mistletoe, hiding among the other trees.'

They trod slowly up the stone steps. It wasn't far to the viewing platform. He carried on telling Mitsuru this and that, though he wasn't sure she was listening.

'This camera has what's called a GN Nikkor lens on it. See how compact it is? Perfect for taking on a hike.'

He held the lens out to show her. She gave it a brief glance.

'Like this,' he continued, pointing at the strap running diagonally across his chest. 'Want to try taking some photos? I'll take care of all the settings, so you won't have to worry about the focus or anything. Just put whatever you want to photograph in the frame and snap away.'

He adjusted the camera so that it would focus wherever she pointed it, then held it out for her.

'Here.'

Mitsuru, more intrigued now, peered at the camera. He looped the strap around her neck. In her hands, the camera suddenly looked a lot bigger. She looked through the viewfinder, pointing it this way and that. He guided her fingers to the shutter release and winding lever, and she began taking photos – at first tentatively, but then with growing enthusiasm.

Hirasaka arrived at the viewing platform slightly ahead of Mitsuru. He turned to find her taking his photo as she made her way up the steps. He gave her an enthusiastic wave. 'Almost there now. Well done!'

There was a family already at the viewpoint. A young girl had placed her hand on a round rock in front of her, and was yelling at the top of her voice.

'*A teacher!*'

Next, a boy who looked like her older brother followed her lead, placing his own hand on the rock and yelling: '*An astronaut!*' Then: '*Or someone at NASA!*'

'Hey, you're not allowed to say two!' said his sister. The boy grinned.

'Let's hope your dreams come true. As long as you study hard and always do your homework, I'm sure they will!' said their mother, stroking them both on the head.

'NASA, huh?' chuckled the father as he snapped a photo. 'You've got your work cut out for you.'

The family started taking photos of each other against the picturesque backdrop of the valley below. Hirasaka would have liked to offer to take one for them, but to the family, he and Mitsuru were completely invisible.

The family set off back down the trail, and silence descended once more.

Just in front of where they had been standing was the smooth rock the children had been touching. It was large – about the size of a squatting adult.

Nearby was a sign explaining that if you placed your hand on the rock and yelled loud enough for it to echo, your wishes would be granted. The children must have been shouting what they wanted to be when they were older. One part of the rock had been polished to an even greater shine by all the hands that had touched it over time. Hirasaka thought about all the dreams that must have been shouted from this spot.

'Mitsuru, look at this. You're supposed to put your hand on this rock and shout out your dream job. If you hear an echo, that means your wish will be granted!'

But Mitsuru stared down at her feet in silence.

'I don't want to,' she murmured eventually, shaking her head. 'There's no point.' She looked up at him. 'What about you?'

'Me? You mean, erm, what would *I* like to be?'

She nodded.

'Well, what I *wanted* to be was . . .' he began, trying to think of something suitably impressive and enlightening.

But nothing he could think of felt true. In the end, he remained silent.

What had he wanted to be? What had he wanted to do?

The truth was, he was still searching.

'To be honest, I still don't know. I turned up at that photo studio not knowing, you see.'

There was a pause. They gazed at the view in silence.

'But . . . I think I might have just figured it out. What *I'm* supposed to do, I mean.'

He laid his hand on the rock. It was impossibly smooth to the touch, so smooth that he never wanted to let go. He thought of all the people who had laid their hands on this rock, and the hope that must have filled their hearts.

Hirasaka made his wish. He didn't shout it out, but he made it all the same.

From the platform they had a sweeping view of the landscape. The kids playing in the park below looked tiny now, and their clothes and the equipment were so colourful that the whole scene resembled some kind of vibrant miniature. Some of the kids seemed to be playing tag, while others were skipping with a large rope. There was something endlessly watchable about the sight.

Mitsuru was taking it all in through the camera's view-finder. Seeing the hesitant look on her face, he told her: 'Take as many as you like.' She began snapping away.

The breeze felt pleasant on their faces.

Hirasaka held up both hands to his mouth like a megaphone. 'Well, let's see if this works . . .'

Mitsuru stared curiously at him.

'Aaaah!' he yelled. Mitsuru looked startled.

Aaah-aaah-aaah, came the faint echo.

'Hear that? Now you have a go.'

But the noise that emerged from Mitsuru's mouth was barely more than a murmur.

'Try shouting from your belly. It feels good to let it all out, I promise. Go on!'

'Aah!' she said, her voice stronger now.

'Louder!'

'Aaaaah!'

Aaaah-aaaah-aaaah, came Mitsuru's echo. She smiled slightly, excited by the sound of her own voice.

'Feels like you're letting everything go, doesn't it? Even things you're unhappy or worried about. Like this . . .'

Hirasaka yelled again.

'Aaaaaah!' cried Mitsuru, imitating him.

'That's it! Come on. Louder, louder!'

She let out her loudest yell yet. He could see the sweat beading on her forehead.

Mitsuru chuckled. It was the first time Hirasaka had seen her smile.

She got out the chocolate they'd brought, tore through the foil, and began munching away.

'Hey, easy on the chocolate. You'll get rotten teeth!'

'I won't!'

On the way back from the viewing platform, Mitsuru seemed a lot more relaxed. They even managed a bit of conversation.

On the other side of the woods they could see the children playing at the park. Under the trees, fallen leaves lay in mounds. Hirasaka poked at one of them with the tip of his shoe.

'Hey, Mitsuru, could you help me gather some leaves? I bought us a sweet potato at that convenience store. I'll show you how to bake it.'

Mitsuru began excitedly gathering fistfuls of dead leaves. Soon she had formed a large pile.

Hirasaka washed the sweet potato, then wrapped it tightly in foil.

'You have to make sure there are no gaps, otherwise it'll burn.'

Mitsuru checked the foil around the potato, then inserted it into the mound of leaves. She stared down at it, as if wondering how on earth they were going to light a fire.

'I don't smoke, so I don't have a lighter or anything on me,' said Hirasaka. Mitsuru's face fell. 'But don't worry. I'll show you how to get a fire going.'

Hirasaka detached the lens from the camera, widened

the aperture, and used it to create a circle of focused light on the ground.

'See if you can find some nice dark leaves for me. The darker the better.'

Mitsuru did as she was told and fished out some leaves that had turned almost black.

'Put those down there. Now watch this.'

He directed the light from the lens onto the pile of leaves. Once he had turned the circle of light into a tiny dot, smoke began rising from the leaves.

Mitsuru let out a gasp of excitement.

'A lens can help start a fire even when you don't have any matches or anything. And if you don't have a lens, you can always use water in a plastic bag.'

Using a branch, Hirasaka drew a picture of a plastic bag on the ground, showing how it could be used to focus the sunlight.

'Really?'

'Really. All you have to do is focus the light in one place. Go on, you have a go.'

He handed the lens to Mitsuru and watched her try. Soon enough, smoke was rising from the spot she'd chosen.

'Wow, it really worked!'

'See? Just focus the light. And remember, black things burn easiest. Oh, and the fire will still be weak when it's just getting going, so . . .' He reached into his pocket.

'You know this fluffy stuff you sometimes find in your pockets? It burns really easily. Watch what happens when I hold it up to the smoke.'

As he did so, the smoke grew thicker.

'You build the fire up, nice and steady, and once it gets going like this, you can blow on it or fan it, too. The flames are stronger now, you see?'

The pile of fallen leaves began burning, and before long the fire was roaring. When Mitsuru leaned in close to blow on the flames, she started choking on the smoke.

'You alright?' asked Hirasaka. 'Try not to breathe in too much smoke – it's bad for your lungs! Listen, just in case you're ever faced with a real fire, the best thing to do is to cover your mouth with a wet cloth. Remember that, okay?'

'Okay,' nodded Mitsuru.

The bonfire kept burning. Hirasaka sat down next to Mitsuru and gazed at the dancing flames.

When the fire had burned down a little, he poked around in the embers with his stick. When he found the large sweet potato, he thrust the stick through the middle of it. It was soft and cooked all the way through.

'Alright, time to eat!'

He tore the sweet potato, still in its foil, into two equal parts, and blew on them to cool them down.

They each took a bite. It was just as sweet and flavourful as Hirasaka had hoped.

'It's so yummy,' murmured Mitsuru.

She reached for the camera at her side, apparently eager for a shot of the baked sweet potato.

'It won't focus properly if you're too close. Try taking it from about *this* far away,' said Hirasaka, holding up his hands to show her the appropriate distance.

Mitsuru took three steps backwards, then took a photo of the sweet potato on top of the dead leaves. Then she turned the camera in his direction, grinning shyly. 'Can I take your photo?'

'Of course!' said Hirasaka, a smile rising to his own lips. He heard the shutter click.

'Once we've finished these, we can head back to the studio, and I'll develop those photos you took. We can look at them together, okay?'

Mitsuru looked delighted by the suggestion. 'Okay!'

He held out a hand, but Mitsuru still seemed a little hesitant.

'Suit yourself,' he chuckled, and began walking. But a moment later, he felt Mitsuru gently clasp his hand.

———•———

They had only taken a few steps when they found themselves back in the photo studio. Mitsuru glanced around in surprise. She was still holding his hand.

'Well, let's have a look at those photos.'

He rewound the film, opened up the back of the camera, removed the cartridge and showed it to Mitsuru.

'Are my photos in there?' she asked.

'Yes, but we can't look at them properly like this. We need to turn them into proper photos. We'll put the film in this special tank, then add some chemicals to develop it.'

He showed her the developing tank – a stainless steel cylindrical container – as well as the reel for winding the film, also made from stainless steel. Mitsuru's curiosity appeared to be piqued.

Hirasaka turned off all the lights in the darkroom, wound the film onto the reel and placed it inside the developing tank. Then he turned the lights back on. Mitsuru blinked. When he handed her the developing tank, it looked big in her hands.

Together, they poured the chemicals into the tank, sealed and shook it and left it to rest, before repeating the procedure. Mitsuru seemed to eagerly await each of his instructions.

'Great, shake it for ten seconds . . . Now let it sit!'

Next, they washed the film, then removed it from the reel. Mitsuru's photos had appeared in the frames.

'There they are!' she exclaimed.

Next, they took a short break while they waited for the film to dry.

'We still have plenty of work to do. The next step is enlarging it and exposing it onto a larger piece of paper.'

'Exposing it?'

'Basically, printing it onto the paper so that it becomes a photo. Can you help me choose which one to enlarge?'

A little bashfully, Mitsuru pointed at the close-up of Hirasaka eating his baked sweet potato.

'Right then, let's get printing. I'll need to darken the room again,' said Hirasaka, switching the lighting to an amber-tinted safelight. With a monochrome print like this, dim light wouldn't affect the exposure.

Next, he shone a light through the negative. To Mitsuru's excitement, the projected image showed up perfectly below it.

Under the orange glow of the safelight, Hirasaka laid the photosensitive paper in position.

'Now I'm going to shoot the light through the negative onto this special paper. Watch!'

Mitsuru watched nervously, waiting for the light to come on.

A brief flash of light passed through the film. But the photo paper below was just as white as before.

'Huh?' said Mitsuru. 'There's nothing there.' All she could see was a white sheet of paper.

'Just a moment . . .' said Hirasaka, plunging the photo

paper into the developing solution. 'Now, keep your eyes peeled!'

A few seconds later, Mitsuru stared in astonishment as the image slowly formed on the photo paper.

'It appeared out of nowhere!'

'Amazing, isn't it?'

Mitsuru nodded.

Finally, he placed the photo paper in a tray and began rinsing it with water. He could just make out his own face, looking up at him from the photo.

The sweet potato had somehow ended up outside the frame, but you could see the steam from it, drifting past his smiling face. His eyes were creased, and he looked genuinely delighted to be tucking into something so delicious. He hadn't even known he was capable of a smile like that. Every leaf on the tree behind him seemed to gleam with its own light. The entire leisurely afternoon they'd spent in the park seemed somehow embedded in that one image.

'You know, Mitsuru, you took a really great photo,' he said. She nodded happily.

After they had left the darkroom, he turned to her. 'Thanks for all your help. Do you mind waiting here while the photo develops?' He gestured towards a stool.

Mitsuru nodded and did as he'd asked. Her feet dangled from the stool, not quite reaching the floor.

'It won't take long. Oh, I know – I'll make you some sweet kinako milk. It's tasty, I promise. You could do some origami while you wait . . .'

Mitsuru sat facing away from him, her thin neck visible beneath her close-cropped hair. She was staring down at her hands as if fervently praying for something.

Hirasaka whisked the kinako powder, sugar and hot milk around in a mug. A cloud of fragrant steam rose from the surface of the drink.

'Here you go,' he said, setting it down on the table. Mitsuru beamed.

She reached for the mug – and then there was a crash, as it shattered on the floor.

'I'm sorry . . . I'm sorry . . .' she repeated, frantically trying to scoop the shards up. Hirasaka noticed that her hands had begun to turn transparent.

'Don't worry, it's fine,' he said, reaching out to hold her hand. But his fingers passed right through her.

Mitsuru was becoming fainter by the second.

As she faded away, she cried out: 'Mister! Help!'

'Don't worry! Mitsuru, you'll be fine, just remember . . .'

As Hirasaka spoke his final words, Mitsuru lost consciousness completely. All she could feel was a darkness swallowing her up.

——— • ———

Where am I?

As Mitsuru opened her eyes, a shudder of pain ran through her body. When she tried to move, she heard the rattle of the chain attached to her leg.

So she was back on the balcony. Weakly, she closed her eyes again.

The balcony was hemmed in by abandoned apartment blocks, and hardly any light made it down this far. Mitsuru had been chained up there since the night before.

She could feel something stuck to her forehead. When she touched it, she felt a sharp pain across her brow. It seemed that the substance in question was dried blood. Halfway through last night's beating, she'd found herself floating up to the ceiling, so her memories of it were a little hazy.

Her stepdad had bent over her and started punching her as hard as he could. Over and over. But she'd been up on the ceiling, watching the scene from above, like it was someone else being beaten. Her mum, meanwhile, had been glued to her phone on the other side of the room.

'Hey, don't overdo it,' her mum had told him, without even looking up. 'You were a bad girl, okay, Mitsuru? Be good next time.'

By the time her stepdad, complaining that his hands hurt, went to fetch his golfclub from the corner of the room, she was too weak to even try and escape. The guy wasn't a golf player. He'd picked it up somewhere for the express purpose of hurting her.

It didn't matter what he chose to beat her with. She didn't care any more. She just wanted the pain to stop.

The kennel, on the balcony, between the rubbish bags: that was where she spent most of her time. He'd kicked the dog too, until it died. Apart from the blanket covered in dog hairs, there was nothing to protect herself with.

Whenever he started 'disciplining' her like that, she'd let her mind float up to the ceiling, and pray for it all to be over. Everything. Whatever it took.

Thrown out onto the balcony, her heels had been the last part of her to clatter onto the floor. She remembered the chain being attached to her leg, and the distant sound of the door to the balcony being locked. When she'd opened her eyes a crack, she'd seen that it was her mum locking the door.

'Sit out there and think about what a bad girl you've been.'

She'd known that it was no use crying to be let back inside, and that nobody else lived in this building and her screams would go unheard. Spring was still some way off, and she remembered shivering as she clutched the blanket to herself. Cold rain had come dripping through the holes in the kennel roof, seeping into the blanket and her shaven hair. She just didn't care any more.

Then she'd blacked out – and found herself in a dream.

She'd been playing with someone. A nice man.

Now she was back on the balcony. Her eyes were so swollen that it hurt to open them, but she managed a squint.

Unexpectedly enough, she could feel sunlight on her face. The balcony faced right up against the building opposite, so that there was only the thinnest crack of sky overhead. But right now, the sun happened to be directly overhead.

It was dazzling.

Just as she closed her eyes, something sparkled in the corner of her vision. She glanced over and realized that it was reflected sunlight.

The balcony was filled with all sorts of rubbish – bags filled with convenience store packaging, plastic containers, newspapers, magazines, egg boxes, flyers . . . Water had gathered in those bags of rubbish, and now glistened in the sun.

She closed her eyes, and wished she could have another nice dream. Maybe I'll get to play with the nice man again, she thought.

That sweet potato had been so delicious. She couldn't even remember the last time she'd eaten in real life. All she could smell here was the rotting rubbish.

Her eyes snapped open.

A fire . . .

She felt like she was about to remember something important.

Get a fire going . . .

It was all coming back to her now.

I'll show you how to get a fire going . . .

That was it. She could hear his voice clearly now.

If you don't have a lens, you can always use water in a plastic bag.

Water in a plastic bag.

Just sitting up sent so much pain racing through her joints that she cried out loud. She stretched desperately towards the rubbish, but the chain around her leg meant she couldn't quite reach. Eventually she managed to lunge forward and grasp a stick, which she used to gradually pull one of the rubbish bags towards her. By the time she had grasped it, her head and shoulders felt like they were about to split apart with pain. She felt a wave of nausea.

The transparent rubbish bag was brimming with the rain that had fallen the previous night.

The light . . .

Focus the light . . .

Focus the light in one place . . .

And remember, black things burn easiest.

Mitsuru flipped through a discarded magazine until she found a dry patch that was printed black.

She focused the light on the black patch.

After a while, a wisp of smoke began to rise.

Mitsuru screwed her eyes shut, desperately trying to remember what the man had said next.

That was it. The fluff in his pocket.

Her clothes were drenched, but there was dry bedding in the kennel. She managed to scrape some lint from the bedding.

The smoke gradually intensified. Soon a small flame had formed.

'Fire . . .'

She sheltered the flame with her hands, carefully coaxing it into life. By gradually adding whatever dry scraps she could lay her hands on, she managed to make the fire bigger and bigger, until it began to roar. Now the flames were licking at the walls. Sparks leapt from the fire with a crackle.

Burn it.

Burn it all.

Burn this stupid place to the ground.

Mitsuru began coughing from the smoke, and held her rain-soaked blanket over her mouth.

Gazing at the blaze from where she lay, she thought to herself, happily, that it was all over.

Her mum and stepfather had both taken their strange medicine, and would still be fast asleep.

The fire grew and grew, enveloping the walls, until it seemed like it would reach all the way up into the sky.

It was hot, but Mitsuru didn't care any more.

Still . . .

What was it the nice man had said at the end?

As she was leaving, he'd desperately tried to tell her something.

Screwing up her face against the heat of the encroaching blaze, she tried her best to remember.

The nice man had looked right into her eyes. He'd smiled and told her it would be okay. Then, he'd said . . .

Just remember to shout.

That was it.

So Mitsuru shouted. She shouted as loud as she could.

Shout. In your biggest, most impressive voice. Remember all that practice we did together.

Just like they'd practised, she drew a deep breath, sucking the air right down into her stomach. She cupped her hands around her mouth.

There we are. Go for it, Mitsuru.

'Aaaah!'

You can do it, Mitsuru. Open your mouth as wide as you can. Just like on the mountain.

'Aaaahhhh!'

She could hear other voices by now.

'Hey, is that building on fire?'

'Quick, call the fire brigade!'

'But . . . does anyone even live there?'

'Just call them, okay?'

'I don't think there's anyone in there. Let's just film it. We can sell the footage to the news or something.'

Now Mitsuru sat up. Her body was screaming with pain. Her knees felt like they were going to give way. She grabbed a bag of rubbish and, leaning on it for support, slowly began raising herself up.

Her head was spinning. She hadn't eaten anything in so long. Still, she didn't give in.

She stood up.

With the blaze at her back, Mitsuru summoned the loudest, most impressive voice she could muster – and screamed.

———

'Hey, there's a kid up here!'

Whoever was shouting, it seemed they were struggling to climb up to the balcony. She could hear voices encouraging her from below.

'The fire engine will be here soon. Hang in there!'

'Keep your head low. Cover your mouth with something!'

Before long, a firefighter had climbed onto the balcony.

'You alright, kid?'

As he picked her up, the cloth that had been covering her face fell away, and she heard him gasp. He must have seen her swollen features, the bruises all over her body, the manacle around her leg.

'I'll get this off you right away. Don't worry, kid. You're safe now.'

When he'd managed to cut through the chain, the firefighter clutched Mitsuru's bruised body and made his way down the ladder, patting her over and over on the head. His voice was choked with tears.

Mitsuru looked back at the apartment, now consumed by flames.

Let it burn, she thought.

'Is there anyone else in there?' asked the firefighter.

For a moment, Mitsuru didn't know what to say.

Let it all burn. That place. That awful man. And Mummy, who never tried to save me from him. Let it all go up in flames.

Mitsuru knew that all she had to do was say there was no one else inside, and that would be the end of it.

And yet she couldn't stop the words that came tumbling from her mouth.

'Mummy. My mummy's in there.'

———•———

The clock on the wall had stopped still. But, thought Yama the delivery man, somehow that was better than no clock at all. It added a certain something to the room.

While he waited for his cup of tea, Yama gazed at the framed black-and-white photo of Hirasaka on the counter. It showed him smiling against a leafy backdrop. It was the only photo the man had left.

All he'd done, Hirasaka had claimed, was play with the kid and teach her a few tricks, so technically he hadn't breached the rules. In any case, thought Yama, the guy had done a pretty great job of skirting the absolute limits of what was acceptable.

Yeah, he'd really pulled a fast one on them.

Apparently, the photo had been taken while he was enjoying a baked sweet potato at a park. He'd broken the ultimate taboo: altering someone's destiny. As a result, all the photos of his own life – all his memories, in other words – had been burned without a trace. And for a guide like Hirasaka, memories were his only real possession.

'Tea's ready,' came Hirasaka's voice from the other room – brimming, as always, with kindness.

When Yama had heard all Hirasaka's photos were going to be burned, he'd secretly saved this one, which happened to still be in the darkroom at the time.

Hirasaka hadn't led a particularly exciting life, it was true. Introverted and single, he'd had few friends and no real hobbies. Rather than the hero of the game, he was like one of the characters wandering around in the background, there to add a bit of colour to the scene more than anything else. No stirring accomplishments or feats of valour. A life lived well out of the spotlight. The undistinguished existence, in other words, of a man who'd never expected to amount to much, and never had.

Still, thought Yama, I'll always remember what he did. I'll remember him as a hero – one who saved that poor kid from her awful fate.

Hirasaka poked his head through the doorway.

'You alright in here?'

'Oh, I'm fine,' replied Yama. 'Let's have that tea. You always brew it just right, you know.'

What about the kid who took the photo, thought Yama? What kind of beautiful life would she lead? What photos would she leave behind?

Hopefully, she'd accumulate so many memories that when she came back here, she'd say: *Just one photo for every year? How do you expect me to choose?*

Yes, one day they'd meet again, thought Yama. But he hoped that day was as far off as possible – far, far off, in the distant future.

———•———

Damp leaves covered the stone steps, and the air was thick with the distinctive smell of the forest. Out of all the times of year to go hiking, there was something about March, when there was still a slight chill in the air, that Mitsuru really loved.

Why was it that, with every step she took towards the summit, her mind felt so much clearer? Was it because she was slowly edging closer to the blue sky above?

Sixteen years had passed since that day. She was a lot bigger now, and in much better shape.

On the sixteenth of March, sixteen years ago, she'd said those words: *My mummy's in there.* Even now, she still wondered from time to time whether she should have said them. But if she hadn't – if she'd told the firefighters there was no one else in the apartment – that decision would surely have haunted her too. Dilemmas like this, where there was no right answer, made her sometimes wonder if the universe actually got a kick out of messing with people.

A fire of unknown origin that ended up exposing a case of horrific abuse; a child's life saved by a series of lucky coincidences. That had been the story, at least. They hadn't asked her too many questions about what started the fire. She'd simply told them that by the time she noticed, the blaze was unstoppable.

Her mother and stepfather hadn't just beaten her on a daily basis; they'd shaved all her hair off and chained her up on the balcony in the middle of winter. If it hadn't been for that freak fire, she would have almost certainly died. The shocking story had been plastered all over the news channels in the wake of the incident. There were close-ups of the balcony of the abandoned apartment. People had been filled with anger at the sight of the rickety kennel in the corner. In interviews, local residents had cried and raged at what had happened.

After the incident, her mother and stepfather had been given prison sentences, while she, Mitsuru Yamada, had grown up in an orphanage in the countryside, where she'd received extensive counselling. She'd never seen her mother again.

To protect her from being associated with the incident or hounded by the press, her name had been changed from Mitsuru to Michi – written with the characters for 'beautiful' and 'knowledge'. Over the past sixteen years, the new name had grown on her. Deep down, though, she'd always be Mitsuru.

Mitsuru!

Her memory of that dream, of that voice calling out to her, had faded and blurred over the years. Now only fragments remained.

Mitsuru had her heart set on a certain job. Maybe it wasn't the natural choice for someone with such a complicated past. Or maybe that was precisely why it appealed to her.

She wanted to be a nursery teacher.

She'd gained a degree in preschool education, and had recently started working at a prestigious nursery school that had just marked its seventieth anniversary.

She was still learning the ropes, really. Sometimes her motivation deserted her, and sometimes she messed things up badly. She didn't always know how to act around the kids, which made her anxious. For some reason, whenever the strain got too much, she found herself wanting to go hiking. A rucksack on her back, and a camera slung over her shoulder. Just her and the mountain.

When she'd moved to Tokyo for university, she'd been pretty strapped for cash, and ended up buying most of her furniture and other necessities from thrift shops. That was where she'd stumbled across the camera. She hadn't been planning on getting one but, feeling strangely drawn to it, had ended up buying it on the spot. Unusually enough for this day and age, it was a film camera. A Nikon F3, with a tiny GN Nikkor lens.

It was a combination she liked. Out hiking, she'd snap away at whatever caught her eye. The stump of a tree, or the last red berry left on a branch. Small things. Beautiful things.

As her interest in photography grew, she'd even started using a rental darkroom. Working away under the red safelight, she'd lose track of time, and all the worries swirling around in her head would gradually settle, like so much mental sediment, until finally she felt at peace.

Now, tying her shoulder-length hair back, she slowly ascended the mountain path.

Amid the otherwise bare branches, she noticed several round clusters of leaves. Mistletoe, she thought as she snapped a photo.

She watched as three birds took flight and soared into the clear sky.

The cry of another bird pierced the limpid air. Mitsuru stopped and listened carefully for its echo. Nearby, a wild cherry tree bloomed gracefully. Framing its pale petals against the blue sky, she pressed the shutter again.

The leaves felt soft, almost fluffy, underfoot. Spotting an unusual fungus by the side of the trail, she leaned in to get a closer look. It was the kind known as a 'monkey's seat' because of its round, flat appearance – although, she thought, it would have to be a pretty tiny monkey.

Arriving at the summit, she found her usual rock – the flat one, with a beautiful view. This was where she always liked to stop for a few sips of tea.

Today, someone else had got here first. A teenage boy – probably about to start senior high school, she reckoned. When she climbed up onto the rock, he bowed slightly at her the way kids his age usually did, then moved down so that he was sitting at one end of the rock. When she sat down, she found it pleasantly warm from the sun.

They sat there in polite silence, each occupying one end of the rock. Mitsuru thought to herself that they must look pretty funny.

'Hi,' she ventured.

'. . . Hello,' came the timid reply.

As they got chatting, she learned that he lived nearby and, as she'd guessed, had just finished his final year of junior high school. He'd managed to get into his first choice of senior school, and was all set for the next chapter of his life.

Mitsuru rooted around in her rucksack and eventually produced a paper bag.

'Baked sweet potato. Fancy a bite?'

The boy hesitated, then smiled. 'Umm, yes, please.'

She split the potato in half, and they sat there munching away.

There was something pleasing about the sight of the boy sitting there on the rock eating the sweet potato. So she decided to ask.

'Taking photos is sort of a hobby of mine.' She gestured to her camera. 'Would you mind if I took yours?'

'Umm . . . I . . .' mumbled the boy. 'My spots are pretty bad right now.' He seemed unsure what face he was supposed to pull.

'Just carry on eating the potato like you were before. You won't even notice me taking the shot.'

'Oh. Okay,' said the boy, looking away from the camera.

Mitsuru smiled, then framed the boy in her viewfinder. *Sweet Potato at the Summit*: not bad as titles went, she thought.

Gazing at him through the camera, she seemed to freeze.

'Erm, have you taken it yet?'

The boy's voice brought her back to her senses. She hadn't even noticed that he'd finished eating the sweet potato.

What was the strange quiver of emotion she'd just felt? That vague, warm wave of nostalgia . . . ?

'Do you always come up here on your own?' she asked.

'Every now and then.'

'Like, when you're worried about something?'

The boy gave a shy smile and nodded.

'Me too.'

Mitsuru squinted her eyes against the gentle breeze. The trees were quietly rustling.

She took a sip of tea and looked up, through the steam issuing from her canteen, at the mountains in the distance. The boy, too, seemed to be quietly savouring the sweeping view, occasionally drinking from his own canteen.

'Beautiful, isn't it?' she said.

'Yes. Very.'

'Have you ever tried shouting from up here? I find it really calms me down.'

The boy nodded.

Whenever she felt crushed by sadness or fear, there was only one thing to do.

Shout.

If the man in her dream had taught her one thing above all else, it was hope. The ability to keep bouncing back. To keep raising her voice against the madness of the world.

Shout, Mitsuru.

Mitsuru stood up.

Then she cupped her hands around her mouth, looked out across the rolling landscape, and took a deep breath.